His Sycamore Sweetheart

STACEY WEEKS

ISBN: 978-1-7779587-8-7

Grace and Love Publishing

Subscribe to Stacey's newsfeed and get the exclusive subscriber story: A Sycamore in the City

Download from StaceyWeeks.com

When spicy peppers and jalapeño mix, anything can happen.

Addison avoids visiting the city. He hates the crowds, traffic, and pace. He especially hates the compact vehicle the rental company insists he'd reserved. But then he runs into Sarah. Or, more accurately, she runs into him, mixing spicy peppers and jalapeño with burnt metal, petrol, hot pavement, and her desperation to not merely survive life in the city but find a place to thrive. Addison isn't looking for a weekend thrill or a romantic entanglement anymore than she is. They both want to go home. Maybe, together, they'll find their way.

Praise for The Sycamore Standoff

Weeks is a writer I count on for sweet contemporary romances with faith messages to make me think. Sycamore Standoff combines sympathetic characters with heartening takeaways about the freedom of living in grace and the power of community.

— AUTHOR EMILY CONRAD

The town of Sycamore Hill is warm and welcoming. The heart of God shines throughout the story. I really enjoyed The Sycamore Stand Off.

— JULIA - BOOK REVIEWER,
CHRISTIAN BOOKAHOLIC

One of the things I enjoy about Stacey Weeks' writing is her ability to present a powerful & touching gospel message organic to the story, without it feeling forced or preachy. Instead of stopping an entertaining story for a sermon, Weeks uses the faith-centered elements to enhance the characters' journeys on the page and point to the Source of peace, strength, and courage.

— CARRIE ~ BOOK REVIEWER,
READING IS MY SUPERPOWER

More Fiction by Stacey Weeks

SYCAMORE HILL

To Sweet Beginnings in Sycamore Hill

The Sycamore Standoff

MISTLETOE MEADOWS

Mistletoe Melody

Mistletoe Mission

Mistletoe Movie Star

*Mistletoe Meadows Anthology

(contains all three Mistletoe titles)

STAND ALONE TITLES

Fatal Homecoming

The Builder's Reluctant Bride

In Too Deep

To God, who has done far more for me than I could ask for or imagine.

So, whether you eat or drink, or whatever you do,
do all to the glory of God.

1 Corinthians 10:31

Contents

Chapter One

It could be worse.

Illuminated only by the light of the moon and several strategically-placed motion sensor lights, Gloria Sycamore fisted her hands on her hips. The toe of her three-inch-heeled boot tapped on the asphalt as she surveyed the jam-packed storage unit. Correction—overflowing storage unit. The contents of her life spilled out of the orange, garage-style door. Gloria righted a toaster tipped on its side, and her stomach lurched, just as it always did at the sight of her independence packed neatly into cardboard boxes with the top flaps folded over.

Just folded, not taped.

And neatly was a stretch.

A dot of sweat dribbled down her neck, between her shoulder blades, and over each bump in her spine in its descent. Her long-sleeved T-shirt stuck to her body like shrink wrap, and tendrils of frizzy, blonde hair had loosened from her ponytail, growing fatter and fatter with each passing, clammy second. The post-sunset coolness of the late September evening did little to moderate her inner, raging furnace. Acrylic fingernails one through eight dug into her palms, and nine and ten lay somewhere on the ground underneath her sea of belongings. She stepped around the box erupting with scarves and shoes she'd never wear in a small town as far behind in fashion trends as Sycamore Hill. In three long strides, she reached the open trunk of her car, pivoted, and paced back.

The top half of the storage unit had lots of space, but Gloria didn't have the upper body strength to stack the boxes any higher. She should have waited for Owen. Correction. She had waited for Owen. She'd waited a whole hour. Sixty minutes. Three thousand, six hundred seconds. Now, ninety minutes later, she'd done the best she could, and it still wasn't good enough. It was the tagline of her life. All twenty-four years. Eight thousand, seven hundred and sixty-some-odd days of not being good enough. Her armpits dampened. She'd blame the growing stains on the physical labor. Not her perceived failure.

Owen was the one who'd picked a Wednesday night for her to move her belongings home. When Gloria announced that she'd given up her apartment in the city, Owen assured her parents that he'd help her, and there was no need for her dad to risk twinging his back again.

Okay. Giving up her apartment was a stretch, too. Lost was a bit more accurate. Unable-to-pay-the-rent-when-she-didn't-have-a-job hit even closer to the truth. Evicted, if she was being totally honest. But this wasn't about her failure. It was about Owen's. He said that church meetings happened on Tuesday nights. Wednesday was clear. Wednesday was free. On Wednesday, he'd be all hers.

And in a nanosecond of terrible clarity, she understood what she'd been trying their entire relationship to not think about. Owen would never be wholly hers. Not as long as he was a pastor. He belonged to the church—the only acceptable mistress.

She puffed out a breath that failed to loosen the tension squeezing her chest. If Owen had come, he would have stacked the boxes. Then, she'd have a bit more room and all ten fingernails. But instead of enjoying Owen's dry banter and benefitting from his upper body strength, she paced in front of unit twenty-one, the one that spewed waves of stuff into view of anyone who happened to drive by the fenced-off self-storage business on the outskirts of town. She pressed her lips together until they tingled. What to do, what to do.

The little piggy that went to market jammed against the edge of a box with the word *books* scrawled in black permanent marker on the side. As her toe painfully compressed, Gloria threw her hands out to the sides for balance and knocked over a coat rack. She hopped on one foot and shook out the other, her jerky movements knocking the flap of the closest box open because, of course, she didn't tape that one shut, either. The rhyme scheme from the familiar storybook sitting on top mocked her. *When life pours you lemons, think lemonade. When the sun gets too hot, be thankful for shade.*

She could use a cool drink of lemonade right about now. Her inability to secure a job after her co-op placement at Grander Nursery School ended had necessitated her move back home. Gloria didn't want to feel thankful things weren't worse, because right now, as she wondered who watched her from the vehicle that crawled down the road at a snail's pace, life felt pretty bad. Unfair. Rip-roaringly frustrating. Still, she automatically followed the directions she gave her precious kiddos. Find the good.

Worse would be not having a place to store her things while she temporarily moved back into her parents' home. Worse would be *needing* to live in her childhood home, when instead, she'd chosen to. Sure, the alternative was going into debt and living on credit, but it was still a choice—big difference. Worse would be losing eight more fingernails and adding a headache. Worse would be — She caught her reflection in a mirror leaning against the corner. Frizzy, blonde curls. Skin flushed to the point of blotchiness. Dark circles under her armpits. Worse would be Owen showing up and seeing her like this and deciding that maybe she wasn't the girl for him after all. *No matter how awful or ugly it gets, you can be thankful for something, I'd bet—*

"Need a hand?" Owen Mason's question interrupted the catchy rhyme.

Worse had found her again. And instead of offering her lemonade, she sucked the juices from plain, old, sour lemons. Her mouth puckered.

Despite just thinking—literally three seconds ago—that it was good Owen wasn't here, her body responded positively to his familiar timbre. His words wrapped around her like a hug that she needed to shrug out of. She didn't turn around. She wasn't in a forgiving mood any more than she was in a thankful one.

"I know what you're thinking." She spoke to the wall.

"Do you?"

She heard his smile, and it sanded a tiny bit of the edge off her annoyance. She drummed her fingers on her hips. "You're probably thinking, 'How did such a young and successful woman like Gloria Sycamore end up back in Sycamore Hill, living with her parents?'"

He chuckled. It started low and rumbled like the trolley carts the storage unit provided customers for hauling stuff from the trunk of their cars to the units. Carts she wouldn't have used had Owen shown up on time. The comfort building in her chest cooled a bit. His footsteps dragged along the pavement with a scuffing sound. She could feel him moving closer. It had always been that way with them.

"What else am I thinking?" His quiet question caressed the back of her neck, and she shivered from the warmth of his breath. She tried to hang onto her frustration, but she couldn't stay mad at him. She never could. She leaned into him and further into their game.

"You're wondering if the only reason she came back is because she couldn't get a job."

"Try again."

"You're wondering if she came back because her family lives here."

"Wrong." He loosely wrapped his arms around her middle and tugged her until her back pressed against his chest. If her sweaty dampness bothered him, he didn't show it.

"You're wondering if she is ready for all the changes coming her way."

He dropped a kiss on her temple.

"Because she's thinking those things," Gloria muttered.

"Are those the only reasons she came back?"

This time, steamy warmth tickled her earlobe, deliciously toasting her insides like marshmallows over a campfire. Gloria melted like s'mores. "You're wondering if any other reason drew her back to Sycamore Hill."

"I am." He cinched his arms tighter and rested his chin on the top of her head. They fit perfectly like that. She stood one head shorter, even with heels. She always felt safe tucked into his arms.

"Maybe," she murmured, not voicing the remaining questions that flitted through her mind.

He's wondering if she's pastor-wife material.

He's wondering if his congregation will accept her.

He's wondering if she'll find a new job in Sycamore Hill and stay for good.

He's wondering if they have a future.

He's wondering if she's wondering about those things.

Because she was.

Gloria twisted in Owen's arms and rested her cheek against his chest. The solid throbbing of his heart steadied her. Sure, it was simpler when she lived in the city, but long distance only worked for so long. Still, no one in the city cared who Pastor Owen of Sycamore Hill Community Church dated. Everyone in Sycamore Hill cared. They not only cared, but they held strong opinions. Strong enough that, up until this point, Owen set most of their dates in the city. He came to her. He insisted.

Was that because he shared her unspoken questions?

She inhaled his spicy aftershave until her lungs felt like they'd burst. She briefly held onto his scent before slowly letting the air escape between her tight lips. Regardless of what anyone else thought about her return to Sycamore Hill or her growing romance with Owen, Gloria was home. For better or worse. Gloria had to get some distance from the controversial trial and the hounding journalists that dubbed her *Gloria the whistleblower*. She'd exposed a falsified drug trial connected to Sycamore Hill nine months ago and had to testify at trial as a result. Now that her name had been cleared—finally —she could come home and hold her head high. The only questions that remained were how the courts would punish her former classmate and roommate for her deception and whether the big company, Emergence Pharmaceuticals, would survive the scandal.

"You're trembling." Owen rubbed his hands up and down her back, adding a delightful friction to her stirred-up insides. "Are you okay?"

"Just tired." Tired of interviews. Tired of depositions. Tired of lawyers. Tired of her hero-move mucking up her life. All she ever wanted was a peaceful, quiet existence. But leaving university under headlines that accused her of cheating, starting and finishing her education after a career change to early childhood education, preparing to testify in court, and now dating the well-loved, small-town pastor was anything but peaceful and quiet.

Another forceful exhale lifted most of Gloria's bangs off her forehead. A few sweaty strands stuck like glue. Gloria's parents had raised her to do the right thing, no matter what it cost. And despite being the black sheep of her over-achieving family, that lesson stuck. Better to complicate her life than let the residents of Life House, the vulnerable clients on which Emergence had slated to begin human drug trials, suffer. The women trying to rebuild their life deserved better. Her gaze found the nursery rhyme book cover again.

The rain hits the dirt, and the dirt turns to mud, and it slips, and it slides, and it spreads like a flood.

Her involvement with the case did bring her together

with Owen again, spreading a little sugar on the oozy-doozy mud pie that was her life. She lifted her face to his.

But Owen's gaze wasn't on her. It was tripping over the twenty or so boxes still looking for a spot in her unit. "I thought I told you to wait for me and that I would help you unload?" There was only the tiniest amount of admonishment in Owen's tone, but it was enough to annoy like a fingernail on a chalkboard.

Two broken fingernails, to be more precise.

"I thought you'd be here at seven o'clock."

He chuckled again. Was everything funny to him? "I had a small church emergency. One of the deacons called as I was heading out the door."

The church. By tomorrow, the church would know she was back, and someone was bound to speculate on what it meant for her, Owen, and the congregation. If Gloria's friends were right, the people would pull out their scorecards and begin tracking tally marks. Was she worthy of their pastor's affections? Was quitting the sciences and trading beakers and test tubes for preschool rhymes an acceptable decision? They'd rank her reliability as a witness in the biggest scandal to impact the town, score her clothing choices, and decide on her overall suitability as a small-town ministry wife. Tonight, the match was tied at zero, but tomorrow? That was anyone's game.

Oozy-doozy, indeed.

Gloria pulled out of Owen's arms. Coolness hit her sweaty skin, and her flesh prickled. She yanked a sweater out of a nearby box, snagging the cuff and pulling loose a thread. Great. Just great. Was this her future if things worked out for them? Her waiting for him, him prioritizing the church, her making do on her own, sacrificing fingernails, mental health, and her favorite sweater? Was his delay the result of a preemptive strike from Sycamore Hill Community Church? Were they letting her know where she ranked on the scale of priorities? If they were, it was mighty passive-aggressive of them. But passive-aggressive was the weapon of choice for most church-goers.

She lifted her shoulder in a shrug as if it was no big deal. Really, she couldn't complain about the church needing him. "I managed."

"Did you?" Owen cocked an eyebrow. He twisted his lips to the right, strolled over to the largest box, labelled off-season clothes, and peeked inside. "You have a lot of stuff."

I've not seen a mess that I cannot wrangle, 'till I met this web that I cannot untangle!

There was no way to know if the quirky rhyme applied more to her storage unit or life. "Was it anything serious with the church emergency?" She lobbed out a lame question. A filler. A way to deflect from the things they should have been talking about.

"Only if you call a leaky roof serious, but Jason had to go through it point by point right then. It couldn't wait." Owen made the kind of noise that told Gloria being a pastor wasn't all sunshine and roses. Her compassion spiked a notch until she did the math.

The things that ranked higher in importance than her were phone calls from the deacons, a leaky roof, church business, and some annoyed guy named Jason. Good to know. Her gaze found her book again.

Be true to what's you, be you all the way. They can't take from you what you won't give away.

Chapter Two

Owen and Gloria sat side by side in two worn armchairs that Owen had scored in a second-hand store. He'd purchased the set shortly after Sycamore Hill Community Church had hired him. Somehow, visiting side by side with a coffee in hand put parishioners at ease in a way sitting across from him at his desk didn't. But he wasn't chatting with a parishioner. This was Gloria. The woman he planned to marry. Back in town, Lord willing, for good. Owen wiped his palms on his pant legs.

His head hurt. He'd been up half the night trying to put his finger on what went wrong between them at the storage unit. Gloria never said anything. She wouldn't. She was great that way. But somehow, between her short answers, sideways glances, and tight features, he heard what she wasn't saying. He'd messed up.

They didn't argue or anything. She still gave him a

chaste kiss goodnight on her parents' front porch. But who was he kidding? That rogue woodpecker in sixth grade had pecked him harder than Gloria had less than a dozen hours before. She was unhappy. Or maybe disappointed was a better word. And he didn't like how that knowledge settled over his heart.

Gloria was the last person he wanted to join the disappointed-in-Owen club.

When he woke hours before his alarm, his gut told him to prioritize damage control and take his girl on an early breakfast date at The Muffin Man. After lingering in the café as long as he dared, he ordered their coffee to-go and moved the date to his office. He made a point to be the first to arrive at the church every morning. He wanted people to drive by, see his car out front, and know he was hard at work.

Last night, Owen might have screwed up, but tonight would be different. Tonight, Owen had plans. Dinner. And not just any dinner. "I booked us a table at that fancy hotel restaurant in Grander City that's famous for its desserts, Queen's Court."

Gloria's eyes lit up. "What a treat!"

The reservation alone guaranteed that Owen would be eating soup from a can for the next two weeks, but the delight on her face made the sacrifice worth it.

Gloria's gaze moved over his small office and eventually settled on his messy desk. Her nose crinkled adorably. He'd swiped his sticky notes, stapler, pad of paper and pencil into the top drawer when they arrived, and he relocated a stack of files to a small round table off to his side. There wasn't anything he could do about the musty carpet smell except open a window and pray to the God of heaven that she didn't think the scent leaked from him. Not the most romantic setting in the world. Even he could see that.

"Have things around here improved much?"

He couldn't stop his gaze from bouncing to the door to ensure no one heard Gloria's question. In a lot of ways, it was easier to confide in Gloria about the difficulties of small-town ministry when she lived in the city. The distance gave her perspective. But now that she was back— His stomach churned, ratcheting up his tension.

Don't come off desperate.

"It's been tough, but God is good."

She angled her head to the side in a way that indicated she wasn't fully convinced. But what was he supposed to say? The employment-honeymoon-period had passed, and no one in seminary prepared him for how hard it would be to keep the peace in a church filled with opinionated people. Whenever the majority of the congregation was happy with him, a small segment remained that wasn't, and that segment was usually the loudest. Love thy neighbor didn't breach the church walls as often as he had expected. At least not during congregational meetings like the one last week.

Heat flushed his skin. Two meetings ago, Hank Sinclair, one of the church's charter members, complained that Owen spent too much time in his office preparing his sermons and not enough time with the people of Sycamore Hill. This last meeting, Hank complained that Owen spent too much time with the people of Sycamore Hill and not enough time in his office preparing his sermons. Ethan, a church member and the owner of The Muffin Man, told Owen not to take Hank too seriously, saying that Hank was so old he probably had a picture of Moses in his yearbook. Still, the criticism burned a hole in Owen's vulnerable psyche. But he couldn't tell Gloria that. He was trying to reel in the girl, not catch and release.

The pressure from Gloria's hand on his knee snapped him back to the present moment. She smiled. "It's okay to admit that it's hard."

Owen peeled his mind off Hank Sinclair. Gloria leaned into him the way she used to when they studied for their grade twelve finals together. Ready to encourage. Ready with a word of hope. It sent a surge through his veins. This was why it wasn't good for man to be alone. Like Adam needed Eve, like his recently engaged friend, Eli, needed Meg, Owen needed Gloria.

Because Sunday was coming. It hurtled toward him every seven days, like an asteroid that never missed its target.

"Knock, knock." Suzy Chalkey, Jason's wife, waddled into his office like a duck under the influence.

Without actually knocking.

Again.

Gloria snatched her hand off his knee and entwined her fingers in her lap.

This had to stop. Owen would ask Janet to start work earlier so she could filter his visitors. Suzy was becoming a problem. Scratch that. Suzy *was* a problem.

"Pastor, can you help me unload the pumpkins from the back of Jason's truck? Clara needs them for the kids this Sunday." Suzy pressed her fingers into the small of her arched back. The movement thrust out her very large, pregnant belly. She stretched as wide as she did tall, and as she overextended her body, she looked Gloria up and down with a combination of open curiosity and self-righteous doubt. She sucked in her cheeks until two deep hollows appeared.

"Sure thing." Owen hopped to his feet. He noted the time of his and Gloria's dinner reservation on the notepad on the desk and underlined the words Queen's Court. He gestured for Gloria to join him as he followed Suzy into the tiny church hallway and toward the arched exterior doors.

"Suzy, have you met Gloria Sycamore? She just moved back to town. We went to high school together."

Suzy tossed an interested look over her shoulder. "We haven't met yet, but I saw her at the storage unit last night when I was driving back to the farm."

Did he hear a subtle correction in Suzy's tone?

"Your car was just pulling into the storage unit. Kind of an isolated spot to meet up, don't you think?"

Yup. Correction. One hundred percent. Owen

stretched his forefinger and thumb across his forehead to avoid answering.

Suzy pushed through the doors to the outside, sending the branches of two overgrown bushes rustling. She fingered the tip of a stray branch as she passed, tugging on it just hard enough that it snapped forcibly back into place.

Right. Suzy had pointed them out last Sunday, claiming those eye-level, lower branches were a hazard to children. "Gloria, can you remind me to come back and trim the hedges on Saturday?"

Gloria's eyes widened, but he gave his head a quick shake. Small enough that Suzy missed it but big enough that Gloria got the message. Her mouth slackened. He'd tell her later why his preaching duties included work as the church grounds keepers, janitor, and repairman. Some days, that job description also included keeping Suzy Chalky happy, but he had yet to successfully cross that item off his to-do list.

Their footsteps crunched on the gravel pebbles they called a parking lot. A couple of shingles lay strewn about from the high winds that ripped through the area overnight. Maybe now Gloria would understand why Jason felt the need to detain him and discuss the roof last night. Unfortunately, Owen wasn't a roofer any more than he was a groundskeeper or maintenance man. And since their fundraising efforts had stalled at about three thousand dollars, he foresaw several shingling-for-newbies videos in his future.

A third vehicle had parked beside Jason and Suzy's truck. Owen squinted. Nathan Clarke.

"Morning, Pastor." Nathan tugged a ball cap lower over his head as the threesome approached.

"Nathan, it's good to see you." Owen clapped the young, widowed father on his back. Would it ever feel natural to say and do pastoral things for people years ahead of him in life experience?

Nathan stuffed his hands into his front denim pockets. "Do you know the children's schedule for the fall programs yet? I called yesterday, and Janet said you hadn't finished the calendar. I need to firm up my childcare by the end of today, and it would really help me out to know the church's plans."

Nathan had stopped attending services when his wife died, but he still sent his four children to every program they offered. They even showed up for Sunday school most weekends. Owen suspected that necessity drove that decision more than faith. The man was barely staying afloat and took advantage of all the programs that included child-minding that the community offered.

"I don't yet, but as soon as I help Suzy haul these pumpkins into the Sunday school room, I'll finalize the details and give you a call. Your kids are in the musical, right?" Owen mentally added finalizing the fall schedule to the growing list of things detracting from what he wanted to do (spend time with Gloria) and from what he needed to do (write his sermon).

"Yes, they are." Nathan's eyes drifted over Suzy's

extended belly, and a softness eased the lines on his face. "Let me help."

"Who has the children now?" Suzy massaged her belly in a circular motion. Even while accepting help, the tiniest bit of superiority came out in her tone.

Owen winced.

Nathan's movements hitched for a beat as he rounded the back of the truck and opened the tailgate, hoisting several pumpkins in his arms.

"That's none of our business, Suzy," Owen gently cut in.

"I disagree," she countered. "The safety of children is everyone's responsibility. Breanna is hardly old enough to handle all the kids on her own."

Nathan's jaw clenched, but he held his tongue.

Owen followed his lead. If it didn't bother Nathan enough to address, Owen wasn't about to overreact. Unless Nathan was waiting or hoping that Owen would speak up. He couldn't tell.

Suzy reached through the open driver's side window door and retrieved her water bottle from the cup holder. She took a long drink before turning her attention to Gloria. "Did I hear right? Do you have a reservation at Queen's Court in Grander?"

Owen sucked in a breath so quickly it whistled. Everyone looked at him. He grabbed two of the larger pumpkins. How long had Suzy stood at his office door and listened before announcing herself? "In which Sunday school room would you like the pumpkins?"

"Clara's room, please."

Owen headed for the side door that opened directly into the corridor of Sunday school rooms. Nathan followed suit. When Gloria picked up a pumpkin and hitched to their train, his chest swelled.

Suzy caboosed empty-handed. "Is it a special occasion reservation?"

"Not really." Owen answered, still steaming over her intrusion. Suzy and her husband had only been in Sycamore Hill three years, but that was enough time for them to put down roots in the church, pump out two kids, and feel comfortable enough to ask nosey questions.

"What's Clara doing with the pumpkins?" Gloria slowed her pace until she walked side-by-side with Suzy.

Suzy hands flapped in front of her. "Oh, you know Clara. She has some sort of lesson on how scooping out the guts is like Jesus taking away our sin and carving a face is like the new creation God makes us." Suzy wrinkled her nose like she was about to sneeze out the devil.

Funny. When Gloria crinkled her nose earlier, Owen had found it to be sweet and attractive. When Suzy did it, he felt nothing but irritation. Or maybe it was her disgust over touching pumpkin innards that soured his gut, unless her expression reflected how she really felt about their Lord and Savior's miraculous work in the heart of a sinner?

But Owen didn't say any of that. He never said half of the comments and questions that raced through his mind. If he did, he'd be looking for a new job within twenty-four hours. Instead, he said, "Brilliant."

Although it wasn't really brilliant. It was cute, but it'd been done before. Every fall that he could remember. But he'd say almost anything to steer the conversation away from Gloria and their date. "Why don't you grab a coffee in the kitchen and put your feet up? Jason told me you've been tired this pregnancy. Nathan, Gloria, and I can finish up out here."

Suzy opened her mouth, but he kept talking. "We bought that decaf coffee you suggested. There's a fresh pot ready. You were right. It's good."

Suzy couldn't camouflage her disappointment at Owen shutting her down, but without a gracious way to refuse, she was bested at her own bossy game.

"I'll come get you when we're done," Owen called as she waddled away.

Nathan forcibly exhaled the minute Suzy rounded the corner.

Gloria outright laughed.

Yeah. He felt it, too. It just wasn't very pastoral to express it.

Chapter Three

Gloria didn't remember the last time she'd laughed so hard, and after spending a long afternoon in court testifying, she needed to laugh.

Owen's impersonation of Suzy on a mission to uncover their plans was spot on. Sure, Gloria didn't know the woman, but the few seconds spent in her company were enough to paint a picture. She pinched the bridge of her nose to squeeze off the exit route her carbonated water sought. It fizzed and threatened to spew like a scotch mint in a bottle of shaken diet soda.

Oh, man. She pinched her side—the scotch mint rocket. She'd wowed her preschoolers that day, shooting herself into the realm of hero-teacher-status and prompting a few phone calls from parents looking for clarification regarding the *explosion* at school.

The tension around Owen's eyes had eased, finally lifting around the same time as their dessert arrived.

Their laughter had helped loosen the lines that seemed permanently carved on his forehead, which was the only reason she shoved down the twinge of guilt regarding their banter. For the first time since Gloria moved back to Sycamore Hill, things between Owen and her felt normal. But that could be because they were back in the city having dinner far from his observant town, nosey Suzys, and bossy Jasons. Insecurity jellified her insides, and it squeezed off her gaiety. "Why do you think Suzy wanted to know our plans so badly?"

Owen shrugged. A tiny vertical frown line returned to his forehead. It was just one wrinkle. A single fold to indicate that the smoothness of Owen's youth was puckering toward adulthood on a track parallel to Gloria's. Only Owen's train led to a town named *distinguished* and *respectable*. Gloria's rocketed toward *undesirable* and *old* faster than her famous scotch mint.

The corners of his icy blue eyes crinkled. "The ladies in church, especially the ones who befriended my last girlfriend, are quite—" He lifted his gaze to the ceiling while he searched for the right word "—motherly," he concluded. "I'm still earning back their trust."

Gloria felt her eyes bulge as she emitted a bark of disbelief. It wasn't Owen's fault the Jezebel he previously dated duped the congregation. "You didn't do anything wrong."

He shrugged. "Except show poor judgment, which throws all my decisions into question."

Gloria's confidence buckled. She tried to remember

everything Owen had told her about Jillian, a cheat dressed in dignified clothing. She'd hoodwinked him and the congregation, charming her way into their lives, laughing at all the jokes and hitting all the right notes, enticing them with her smooth words. All the while, she viewed this town as a stepping-stone to bigger things.

Jillian made plans for Owen. She had envisioned a large megachurch future where she filled the role of First Lady. The woman came from an urban setting that was far more city mouse than country mouse and planned to return there with her celebrity pastor on her arm.

Gloria forced her clenched hands to relax. Hot pink nail polish reflected the light from the massive restaurant chandelier—a light that was very much city mouse, hanging over the repaired fingernails of a city mouse that wore a very city mouse outfit while on a date with a one-hundred-percent country mouse man.

Which begged a question. Why did her country mouse constantly plan dates in the city? Gloria swallowed her insecurities. As the similarities between Jillian and her stacked up, she pressed her pink painted fingernails to lips smeared in a complimentary hue of gloss. With cheeks growing hotter by the second, Gloria talked herself down from the ledge. Having the last name *Sycamore* should help the people accept her. Her parents practically founded the town. It almost guaranteed that no one would be outright mean. At least not to her face.

Gloria tugged at the billowy scarf wound casually around her neck. She and Emma Powles had debated the scarf. Gloria had hit it off with the nurse practitioner months ago when the woman snuck into the hospital to find important documents that turned the tide of the Emergence trial. As the prosecuting attorneys prepped them to testify, they'd grown close. They shared common interests, including an appreciation for the occasional impractical item just because it looked stylish. But the loose folds of the draping fabric they'd previously admired now choked off Gloria's oxygen supply. The women of Sycamore Hill Community Church had a stranglehold on Owen, and an exceptional talent for communicating cutting remarks through smiles and pleasantry.

Stop it, she scolded her snowballing thoughts. But she couldn't stop her catastrophizing fears any more than she could stop a snow boulder rolling downhill. Just who did his congregation think they were? They had no right to impose their insecurities about Jillian upon her. No right! And making their pastor pay for the sins of his ex? Totally unacceptable. The bigger the snowball got, the more it riled her up. But instead of expressing her fears and engaging in the kind of open and honest communication two people considering marriage should be able to have, she pasted on the type of insane smile she imagined a suitable pastor's wife would wear, cleared her throat, and said, "Tell me more about the children's programming at the church."

Owen prattled on about the annual fall musical spearheaded by Clara Brisbane. Meg Gilmore, Clara's neighbor and Gloria's friend, had told Gloria about Clara, her sweet grandmotherly neighbor that came to her aid during a break-and-enter a few months back. Gloria looked forward to getting to know the feisty woman that stepped into a motherly role for Meg. Meg and Eli and Owen and Gloria hit it off, and they often double-dated in Grander. They had spent many pleasant evenings together playing board games and watching movies at Gloria's apartment in the city.

"The musical is the only church program that starts in August, before the fall program kick-off, doubling as a late vacation Bible school," Owen said. "They'll perform the musical at the Fall Festival in a few weeks."

Gloria made supportive sounds as she spooned the last bit of her creamy dessert into her mouth. She hadn't eaten all day in anticipation of this evening. The second Owen had mentioned Queen's Court, she started a fast. Not a fast to fit into her new dress, although the dress was totally fabulous, and somehow, putting it on while her empty stomach growled made her feel like it hung a bit more loosely than before. The entire purpose of Gloria's fast was to better appreciate the creamy chocolate mousse currently melting on her tongue with delicious satisfaction. More delightful than waking on Christmas morning to an overstuffed stocking at the foot of the bed. "Did you make arrangements to fix the roof?"

Owen's expression tightened some more. "The roof's going to cost more than I expected. We'll either have to fundraise some more first, or I'll learn how to lay shingles. The fund is about a thousand shy of what we need. It's tarped for now. As long as we don't get another driving rain, it'll be enough."

Gloria had never tasted a dessert so creamy. She tried to keep her attention on Owen, but it was so hard with such delicious goodness overwhelming her taste buds.

Owen.

The roof.

The church.

Right.

"You'll fix it? Don't you already do more to maintain the property than the average pastor?" Owen had never been a handy guy. A pair of unruly bushes that needed trimming on Saturday came to mind. "You know, there was a time when Sycamore Hill Community Church rotated volunteers to maintain the church's exterior property. I remember the weeks the responsibility fell on my family. Dad would trim the hedges while Jessica and I would weed the garden. Mom dusted and vacuumed."

Did Owen remember how he'd join them? He and Gloria would sneak off past the tree line and pick wild raspberries. They'd only been kids, but a tiny clearing hidden from view became their secret spot.

A faint pink washed Owen's cheeks as his attention drifted to the tree line. Oh yeah. He remembered all right. The taste of their first awkward kiss was raspberries and sunshine. "Things changed after they caught my predecessor stealing from the offering."

Her spoon clattered against the side of the bowl, and

the couple at the neighboring table stared at them. She gave a little shrug and mouthed, *oops*. "Between your ex and the former pastor, the past casts a pretty big shadow over your present."

"Hank says that hard, physical labor keeps a man honest." Owen's tone held no humor, contradicting his smile.

The waiter brought the bill. Gloria hated to wrap up the evening, but everything about this relationship needed to be above reproach. She needed to get home at a reasonable hour. She was dating the pastor, after all.

After paying for their meal, Owen held out her jacket. She slipped her arms into the sleeves, and he slung an arm around her shoulders. Gloria leaned into his side. The evening had been everything she had hoped it would be. But as Owen pushed open the exit door, Gloria's heel turned. It caught in the crevice on the cobblestone sidewalk. She teetered into Owen with a gasp and a giggle.

The entire block in this portion of the city had that old-town feel. Gloria adored the cobblestone walks and the Victorian-style buildings with various elements from Italianate and Second Empire. Old town riches in a modern city setting.

Owen steadied her, catching her at the elbows and pulling her to his chest. She lifted her face, her gaze lingering on his lips.

Against such a charming background, the moment turned swoon-worthy. Movie-like. Better than she could have ever hoped. She leaned in closer, and Owen's arms moved from her elbows to her waist. She rolled her bottom lip into her mouth. Then somebody cleared their throat.

Right. They blocked the door.

Owen shuffled them off to the side. "Sorry, I didn't mean—"

"Good evening, Pastor." Suzy's clipped greeting threw cold water on the moment.

Gloria froze. She suddenly saw them as Suzy must. Her fingers splayed across Owen's chest. His arms at her waist. Her giggling and flirting. All the delicious goodness of their three-course dinner solidified into an iceberg in her gut.

"Did you enjoy your *meal*?"

Owen appeared to be temporarily struck mute.

"It was wonderful," Gloria answered.

"At least, I hope you're only here for dinner."

Gloria's smile slipped from her face. She glanced back at the hotel. Suzy couldn't possibly mean . . . The women locked eyes. Suzy knew exactly what she was saying.

Gloria stood there for several seconds, stunned into silence at the tawdry insinuation. The hotel with its intricate design, decorative features, and Victorian influence certainly created the ambiance of a romantic getaway, but Suzy knew Owen. He was always a gentleman, always aware of the image he projected. The gall of her to accuse—

"I assure you that we only had a meal here tonight." Owen finally found his tongue, although his words came out all gravelly and rough. "I hadn't considered how this might look, coming out of a hotel. It's good that you saw us and approached us immediately to clarify things. Another woman might have simply speculated and gossiped. Thank you for your directness."

Thank you? He was thanking the woman for practically accusing them of having some torrid affair? Gloria's face grew hot—hotter than it should be on a cool fall night. Owen dropped one arm to his side and pressed his other hand against the small of her back in a warning. Gloria shored up her tenuous grip on her last shred of self-control.

"Rookie mistake, Pastor." Suzy's smugness and Owen's passivity hurled a few unchristian thoughts through Gloria's mind.

"Now you have the facts. Do you remember Gloria from this morning?" Owen straightened to his full height. "She's Teresa and David Sycamore's daughter. Gloria, you must remember Suzy Chalkey, from church? We helped her with the pumpkins. She moved to Sycamore Hill after you left for university." Owen swayed, and it shifted his upper body even closer to Gloria, making it clear where he'd land if Suzy forced him to pick sides.

That tiny movement almost made up for the polite dance he and Suzy waltzed. Owen might want to pretend their meeting was happenstance, but Gloria wouldn't. She'd spent much of her childhood cowering before alpha-females. The Suzys of her high school had looked down their noses at Gloria. Always judging her. Always finding her lacking because she refused to yield to their whims. It carved a hollow in her soul. Never fitting in. Never being accepted. Suzy's knife twisting reopened the vulnerability.

But she wasn't that little girl with frizzy hair anymore. And she'd known Suzy was trouble the second the woman waltzed into Owen's office without knocking and posed her nosy questions. However random Suzy tried to make this encounter, Gloria knew it had been planned and expertly executed.

"Yes, I remember Gloria." Suzy flicked her gaze to Gloria for the briefest second before locking it back on Owen.

Gloria's gaze trailed over the vehicles parked on the side of the busy street in front of the hotel. Bingo. Parked right across from the window that had framed Gloria and Owen while they ate sat a pick-up truck that looked suspiciously like the one that carted pumpkins to the church this morning. From that vantage point, the woman knew they'd only had dinner, but she felt the need to play out this . . . this . . . Gloria fumbled for clarity. This passive-aggressive power play.

"What brings you to town, Suzy?" Owen's eyes iced over, and Suzy must have felt the temperature dip, because her posture wilted just a bit. "Such a drive at eight months pregnant couldn't have been comfortable in a truck. Is Jason with you? I remember him mentioning his concern for your comfort this close to the end of your pregnancy."

"No, no, I'm here alone." Suzy shifted from offensive to defensive. "I better get going." She shuffled a few steps away and gave a little wave. "See you Sunday, Pastor."

"We'll see you Sunday, Suzy." Gloria answered for Owen and threaded her arm through his.

Owen's breath rushed out as Suzy blended into the crowd and disappeared. "I know we didn't do anything wrong, but somehow I feel like a boy caught with my hand in the cookie jar."

Gloria stared at the spot in the crowd that swallowed Suzy. This was going to be harder than she thought.

Chapter Four

Owen dragged his index finger over his left eyebrow. The slow, methodical action of stretching the skin did little to relieve the churning in his stomach. Gloria sat across from him with such hope in her eyes. Such certainty.

His gaze flicked behind her to the wall where an inspirational Scripture passage painted on white-washed barn board hung.

Philippians 4:6-9, "Do not be anxious about anything, but in everything by prayer and supplication with thanksgiving let your requests be made known to God. And the peace of God, which surpasses all understanding, will guard your hearts and your minds in Christ Jesus. Finally, brothers, whatever is true, whatever is honorable, whatever is just, whatever is pure, whatever is lovely, whatever is commendable, if there is any excellence, if there is anything worthy of praise, think about these things. What you have learned and received and heard and seen in me —practice these things, and the God of peace will be with you."

Despite his internal upheaval, he smiled like he always did whenever he looked at the tableau. After he accepted the role as pastor, he'd looked up old Mrs. Canmore. She had a storied career as an artist and liked to fill her time with odd jobs. A few people warned Owen against hiring her, because the older Mrs. Canmore got, the more mischief she stirred, and she'd never set foot in a church in all her days. But Owen commissioned her anyway to style these verses. He laughed out loud when he came into the office one day to find the old gal hanging a board on the wall that said the peace of God would guard his heart and mind *in Christ's cheeses*. Later, Mrs. Canmore would claim it was an honest mistake, but Owen wasn't so sure.

The twisted memory failed to lighten his mood. God had heard his list of requests, all right. It frequently held names like Suzy, Jason, and Hank. But where was his promised peace? Why did his insides feel like a roller coaster about to shoot off the tracks?

Because I have as much of God's peace as I let myself have. Words from his most recent sermon bit back. This wasn't the first time the difficulty of applying the abstract theology he proclaimed from the pulpit resonated. He understood the message, but what had to change in his life for that truth to bring peace? That bit remained foggy, making him the worst pastor ever.

He rubbed his palm over his gut. If it churned any harder, he'd be producing butter.

What would Gloria think if she knew how difficult it was for him to apply the truth he preached? The question lingered like a bad dream where someone swung open a door to a bank vault and told him to take as much as he wanted, and he left with only a couple of pennies because all he had on was a pair of underwear with no pockets to haul the cash.

This all flashed through his mind in a millisecond while he maintained a pasted smile and fixed his attention on his newest source of turmoil: Gloria.

"Well?" She leaned forward, eyes wide and eager, certain her request wouldn't be a problem.

Except it was.

And therein lay the reason for his discomfort. The woman he loved needed something within his power to provide, but he couldn't. That's right. *He loved her.* He loved Gloria Sycamore, but she was going to struggle to believe it when he said no. He didn't like how the negative word tasted.

Janet's soft movements from the volunteer secretary desk just outside his door trickled through the open doorway, left ajar for accountability. There was no way Owen was giving his congregation the opportunity to gossip about him having a young woman in his office alone. Despite the noises of opening and closing filing cabinets and the clicking of computer keys, he was pretty sure Janet listened to every word. She maybe even kept a loop of women updated as he and Gloria battled it out. She seemed to make a lot of passes across the door while texting on her phone, and she'd offered them coffee three times in twenty minutes. An adolescent temptation to feed her fake intel just to see what she would do with it shot through him.

"It's not ethical for me to write a personal reference for someone I am in a romantic relationship with," Owen explained again.

Gloria blew out a *harumph*.

"What about your teacher from the ECE program? Or the preschool where you completed your co-op placement?"

"She wrote me a referral letter. I picked it up after my appointment with the lawyers wrapped up. But Cathy wants a reference from someone in town, a non-relative that has experience with kids. That's the only way she'll consider me."

Owen knew Cathy Whitmore. Her wire-rimmed glasses and sharp eyes missed nothing. Children liked her plump cheeks and a turned-up nose. There was something wonderfully *grandmotherish* about her, despite her young age. Cathy carried the faint scent of mothballs with her wherever she went. As friendly as Cathy was, she'd always reminded Owen of some twisted version of the movie Freaky Friday, except in this case, Cathy was an eighty-year-old woman forever trapped in a thirty-year-old body. She seemed like the type of person who had always been old even when she was young, but they didn't interact much. She didn't attend his church, and when their paths crossed, she seemed a tad uncomfortable around him. But that was often the way it was once people learned he was a pastor. Suddenly their posture straightened, their language cleaned up, and they felt compelled to justify their spiritual choices.

Gloria's voice dropped as if she was onto Janet's ploys. Owen envisioned Janet holding a paper funnel to her cocked ear. "If I can't get a job, I can't stay."

That hit below the belt. If God wanted them together, God would make a way. But it was easier for him to say that. He had a secure job. "Don't make this about our future. That's not fair. I can't manipulate circumstances to get my way."

Janet walked by the door again. The paper funnel must not be working.

Was that a *tsking* sound from Janet?

Gloria's eyebrows lifted, and the right side of her lip shot up like it'd been hooked and someone had yanked the line. "Ah, you run a Sunday school program."

He shook his head. "That falls under Clara Brisbane's domain. She's been running the Sunday school classes for years. Have you seen her since you've returned?"

It was Gloria's turn to shake her head no. "Meg told me about how important she's become to her, and I remember Mrs. Brisbane from when I was young, but that's it."

"A recommendation from me is a conflict of interest," Owen repeated, more to convince himself than her. "You have to see that."

An *uh hum* rounded the corner. The woman might as well be amening Owen. Verbal affirmations lifted his heart on Sunday mornings but had the opposite effect right now.

Gloria slumped back into her chair. All the joy and excitement drained from her. "It's not. Not really."

His insides cramped. He hated this, but he had to care about appearances, especially since the fiasco at Queen's Court. It came with the job. He was held to a higher ethical standard. But he also wanted to be supportive and encouraging to Gloria, and therein lay the conundrum.

"I suspect Mrs. Brisbane would welcome help in the kid's department," he started gently. "In fact, the musical has turned into a far bigger production than she expected. Why don't I reintroduce you, and if you work with her for a few weeks, she can provide the reference."

A harumph covered by a cough came from outside the office. At least Janet tried to cover her eavesdropping.

Gloria glowered at the open door.

Owen was half-tempted to shout that Janet should take the rest of the day off and go to the doctor to get her throat checked. Anything to let the woman know that he was onto her—but he forced himself to focus on Gloria. One problem at a time. "Volunteering isn't as quick or as neat as getting me to write the reference, but it does serve both our needs."

Gloria drummed her fingers on her thighs.

"Is something else going on?"

She rubbed the back of her neck. "Cathy asked about the trial and why I changed career tracks."

"Isn't it normal to ask questions in a job interview?"

Gloria scrunched her eyes and pinched the bridge of her nose. "That's what Emma said when I told her. But they're gateway questions into the trial against Emergence. I don't know why it surprised me, and I don't know why it bugs me."

Owen's tongue pressed against the roof of his mouth. Of course, Gloria had spoken with Emma about the trial. Emma played a key role in securing the proof Gloria needed to expose the dangerous plan. Owen tried not to look too deeply into why Gloria hadn't confided in him.

When Gloria was accused of falsifying results from her experiments, the university forced her out. Ben, a local reporter Owen had looped in to help Gloria, exposed the truth. Gloria's roommate, Tiff, had framed her. Tiff had been working for the drug company as a student and had been promptly promoted after she graduated. When Emergence was about to begin drug trials on residents of Life House, Gloria came back to town armed with enough evidence to set Ben on the right trail and to clear her name.

But that's where his involvement ended. Gloria hated talking about the ongoing trial. She hated everything to do with that period of her life, proved by the way one innocent question in a job interview burned her chops.

"Did you explain the entire experience is what set you on this new career path to work with children?"

"I did, but she's concerned that once the trial wraps up, I'll head back to the city, and she needs someone long term. Committed."

A part of Owen shared Cathy's concern, but he shoved it back down his dry throat. But no matter how deeply he buried his doubts, one question still managed to push its way to the surface.

Was he enough reason for Gloria to stay? He wasn't before.

He shoved away the memory of the *Dear John* letter she'd left him. When the drug scandal hit the news, Gloria disappeared. She left her family, the town, and him with nothing more than a written good-bye. Who's to say she wouldn't do that again? If things heated up at church, would she have what it took to stay and fight for them?

Owen turned his hands palms up. "Honestly, I don't know what to do. All I can say is that I am trying to make the best decisions I can with the information I have on hand. And right now, a reference from me won't be good for the ministry here and won't be as good for you as an unbiased reference."

"Then Clara it is." Gloria conceded, but it didn't it feel like a victory.

Gloria pulled her phone from her purse and called Cathy. "Is it possible for me to put in some volunteer hours at the church and then hand in a recommendation? It'll take longer, but it appears to be the only way." Gloria's expression hardened as she listened to whatever Cathy said, and her grip on the phone tightened. "Thank you." She hung up and folded her arms across her middle. "She won't hold the position for me, but if it is still available when I have everything in place, she'll consider me."

Owen eyes went heavenward. *Thank you, Lord!*

"It'll work out. You'll see." He inhaled sharply, but the inside of his chest pinched in a way that undermined his confident declaration.

It didn't feel worked out. Not even close.

Chapter Five

J anet walked by Owen's office door again, and twitchiness pulsed in Gloria's extremities. She rubbed a fingertip along the seam of her jeans, distracting herself with the warmth the friction created. She and Owen couldn't dance around it forever. At some point, they had to talk about the church and its impact on Owen's personal life.

At least she thought they did. She didn't know. She'd never dated a guy in ministry before. Yet somehow, she knew today wasn't that day. Today, they'd pretend everything was fine when it wasn't, talking *around* the issue instead of discussing the issue.

A shiver swept over Gloria as if the room temperature suddenly dropped a full ten degrees. She glanced at the window to see if it was hanging open so she could blame her inner freeze on the weather. But no luck. She had no one to blame but herself.

Not Owen.

Not Janet.

It was her. It was always her.

Suddenly, she was a child again. Not quite fitting in. Standing on the outside of the group. Smiling as a teacher commented on having her sister in his class a few years prior. Then, reading disappointment in her teacher when Gloria failed to perform as well as Jessica. Clapping while Jessica accepted another honors award, and indulging her parents while they assured her that her best effort was all they required.

But it wasn't true. There was no award for best effort. There was no honors certificate for a solid B average. Teachers didn't remember average students. And girls with frizzy blonde hair and braces weren't invited to pool parties.

Gloria ran a hand over her hair. The braces eventually came off and she learned to control the frizz, but she still wasn't enough. Suzy made that clear. Janet didn't approve of her. Gloria couldn't remember when the shame of not measuring up wasn't a part of her, making her dirty. Contaminated. Unclean.

Gloria bit the inside of her cheek and tasted blood. There was something about how she felt that asked for blood.

If she had to move for work, her future with Owen would crumble like the remnants of a shack after seismic activity hit a ten on the Richter scale. Yet, he sat there with a goofy grin on his face that implied she was overreacting. Here she was, fighting to save her future, *their future*, and he had the nerve—*the nerve*—to sit there and smile.

Okay, not really smile. But the corners of his lips twitched in that annoying way that meant he was trying *not* to smile, which was just as bad. Maybe even worse. He was *handling* her. Trying to manage her response like she was Janet, or worse, Suzy.

"The job posting has been up for some time." Owen pushed his chair back from the desk and retrieved a light jacket from a nearby hook. "I don't think anyone will swoop in to steal it from you in the next few weeks." He motioned to the office door for her to lead the way out.

Gloria snorted again. Where did he get off saying that with such confidence? It wasn't his career hanging in the balance. She lifted her chin a millimeter and sailed past him and out the door.

Janet called out cheerily, "Heading out?"

Gloria snorted. Janet had probably already called Mrs. Brisbane to report that Gloria was trying to corrupt their dear pastor by asking him to go against his conscience. A slight tinge of disapproval shone in the woman's perky eyes.

First Suzy. Now Janet.

She was oh for two.

This was not how Gloria envisioned meeting Owen's congregation. She'd written an entire Sunday morning scenario in her mind that had the congregation anticipating her arrival like the guests at a wedding. Meg had laughed at her vision. Emma said she was out of her mind. But Gloria imagined that she'd come in on her father's arm, and they'd collectively inhale, convinced that she was the missing piece to Owen's puzzle. Not once in her little dream did she tick off a nosey secretary or deacon's wife. Nevertheless, here she was. Down by two.

Not that any of this would matter if she didn't get the job.

Without a job, Gloria would be forced to move wherever she could find employment. She'd work all week. He'd work every weekend. They'd drift apart, neither of them wanting to terminate the relationship but unable to stop the trajectory of them hurtling toward breaking up. She'd be alone—again. And every time she returned to Sycamore Hill to visit her parents, she'd be forced to make polite small talk with whatever woman Owen eventually settled down with—a woman the congregation wholeheartedly approved of because she didn't wear high heels, or paint her nails bright colors, or ask their pastor to do something he didn't want to do.

Gloria pressed a palm to her heaving belly. It was suddenly difficult to inhale. How could Owen just move on like that? How could he replace her so easily? How could—

"I'm walking Gloria to Mrs. Brisbane's to introduce them. I won't be long," Owen said.

Gloria snapped back into the present. She couldn't

be sure, but she would have sworn that she heard Janet *tsk*.

Again.

Gloria smiled at Janet anyway.

This was why she worked with kids. Working with kids was a million times better than working with adults. Children were one hundred percent honest. Sure, that brutal honesty might hurt. Preschoolers had yet to develop an inner editor. They just spoke.

The small volcano on your chin just popped.

Your belly is nice and soft, just like a pillow.

I can smell what you ate for breakfast.

Brutal, yes. Honest? Always. She'd take that over spun truth and manipulation any day.

For a moment, Owen studied her, looking as though he could read her mind and was considering whether her catastrophizing was worth addressing. Gloria held his gaze until he blinked. He turned to Janet, whose mouth hung slightly ajar as if she was fluent in subtext. "Can you please find me a book about roofing? I want to look into the project a little bit more."

"Yes sir," Janet snapped into action, her fingers clicking away on her keypad as if Owen had just asked her to decipher the final clue in a search for the Ark of the Covenant. "It was nice to see you again, Gloria." Janet didn't look up from her screen. A subtle snub. Like Gloria wasn't worth the time it would take to glance her way. "I hope to see you on Sunday."

And there it was again. *A tone.* A facial tick. Subtext

that almost dared Gloria to try and prematurely claim a spot beside their pastor.

"Oh, I'll be there." Gloria gave a little wave of her hand. "My family never misses a Sunday." But Gloria wasn't stupid. She wouldn't be sitting with Owen. She'd claim her old place in the Sycamore family pew, and that's where she'd stay. The sacred spot beside the pastor was only hers after a ring circled her fourth finger on her left hand. Claiming it prematurely was suicide.

Fifteen minutes later, Gloria and Owen strolled down the street, nearing Clara's house. Gloria tucked her hand into the crook of Owen's elbow. Leaves in various shades scraped along the sidewalk. Maple, ash, and oak mixed and danced in the breeze. All except the sycamore. The sycamore trees hung onto most of their leaves throughout the winter unless a harsh wind of heavy snow blew them free. They didn't usually shed their dead until early spring, until the swelling buds completed the separation. Was Gloria too much like her namesake, holding onto Owen and the hope of a future together, refusing to release him to the ministry until something outside of her control forced her to let go?

Owen squeezed her hand between his elbow and side, tugging her a bit closer.

She gave him a sideways glance. He nodded and smiled at everyone they passed.

"Do you ever get tired of it?"

"Of what?"

She overlapped her long cardigan around her body

and cinched the belt. "Being the pastor. Of everyone having an opinion on your decisions?"

Owen reached for her hand and threaded their fingers. His shoulders lifted and released. "It comes from love."

Her facial muscles tightened. Did it? Or did it come from a need to control?

"After high school, when you left for the city, things in my life got complicated."

The cramping in her face spread to her chest. If complicated scared him, she was in trouble. So far, nothing about her return to Sycamore Hill had been easy, simple, or straightforward. She bled complicated. "How?"

His eyes found hers. "Jillian."

Right. Jillian. The woman they all loved until they didn't.

"Everyone assumed we'd marry."

Unexpected pain stabbed, and agony shot from the point of impact, electrifying every nerve ending in her body. Owen had loved another woman. Owen had proposed. The congregation loved her. Welcomed her. Accepted her. And all Gloria got was a refusal to provide a reference and a stalker named Suzy.

"Jillian wasn't genuine." Owen's attention followed the erratic path of a bird. Was he that taken by the species or was he still grieving Jillian and therefore couldn't bear to meet Gloria's gaze? Was Gloria just—she gasped inter-nally—a rebound romance? Did Owen still have feelings for Jillian? This woman who was, what? An international spy? A narcotics dealer? Secretly married with children? What could have been *so bad* that Owen felt *so grateful* for this second chance from the community that he forfeited his privacy and personal life, granting access to anyone who demanded it?

"Jillian said and did all the right things, but Janet saw her one night at a restaurant in the city. As she approached the table to say hi, she overheard Jillian mocking Sycamore Hill, our country way of life, and boasting about her plans for me."

"And?" Gloria leaned in closer.

"And after welcoming her and showing her kindness, it hurt."

That hardly seemed like a big enough crime to scar the congregation for life.

"She went on for some time about our backward ways and hokey fashion."

Fashion? The clicking of Gloria's heeled boots against the sidewalk grew in volume until they were all Gloria heard. She had agonized over her outfit today. She must have tried on a dozen ensembles, looking up outfits on Pinterest for that perfect combination that said educated and professional but willing to get dirty and play with the kids. She fingered the high collar of the red knitted sweater she layered under a long cardigan. Her painted fingernails perfectly matched. No wonder Suzy and Janet acted as they did. She reminded them of *her.*

Someone should have warned her.

Before Gloria could respond, a howl shouted from behind, "Look out!"

In a blink, Owen yanked her to the side, and Gloria stumbled out of the path of a scooter zipping past them that gravity pulled downhill.

"Sorry!" the girl called as she blurred by them. A girl wearing—Gloria squinted—pajamas?

"Be careful, Breanna!" Owen shouted at her rapidly-disappearing form.

He tightened his hold around Gloria. "You okay?"

A hum of contentment vibrated deep in her chest. She was more than okay.

His arms relaxed around her waist, but he didn't remove them.

She lifted her face to his. She could almost see her reflection in his eyes. Owen was a good man. A kind man. He wasn't letting the church walk all over him. He was being gracious. Showing them mercy because of all they'd endured before him. His gentle nature was one of the reasons she loved him.

The air between them charged. If she leaned in just a little bit more . . . Her gaze dropped to his lips.

Owen cleared his throat.

Just like that, the spell was broken.

"Breanna's probably late for school because she was helping her dad with the twins."

Twins? Gloria's midsection hiccupped. There were only one set of twins in Sycamore Hill. "She's Nathan's daughter?"

"His oldest. Here we are." Owen pushed open a waist-high gate that fenced in Mrs. Brisbane's front yard and motioned for Gloria to go first. A white picket fence gave the property a cozy feel. The homes in this historical part of the town were smaller than Gloria's parents', but they had just as much character.

Owen used the brass knocker on the front door, and Gloria shifted her weight from side to side.

"Pastor Owen! What a pleasant surprise." Mrs. Brisbane opened the door wide.

Yeah, right. As if Janet hadn't called already and prepped her.

"This is my girlfriend, Gloria."

Girlfriend. All her cynicism fled. It was the first time Owen had introduced her that way, and she had to admit it; it sent a thrill tingling from her head to her toes. After all the subtle put-downs, Gloria practically glowed. Owen had claimed her publicly.

"Gloria needs a reference for her application at the preschool, and I suggested she volunteer with you in the children's ministry. Afterward, if you feel it appropriate, you could write her a recommendation."

As Clara Brisbane's gaze moved up and down Gloria, Gloria couldn't help but straighten. Then, the woman did something so completely unexpected that Gloria wasn't sure if she was serious or not.

"Hallelujah!" Clara threw her hands into the air. "Meg and I were just praying the Lord would provide, and here you are. His provision standing at my front door, hand-delivered by God."

God? More like hand-delivered by Owen.

"Come on in, dear," Mrs. Brisbane opened the door even wider and gestured for Gloria to enter. "I have the perfect job for you. My doctor was just telling me that I need to cut back and get control of my diabetes. But how was I supposed to say no to all those kids? They've been working all month on the play. I couldn't just up and walk away."

Gloria stepped over the threshold into Mrs. Brisbane's house as Owen simultaneously stepped back. Her gaze locked on his. He wasn't coming?

"I'll wait out here. I have a few emails to answer." He wiggled his phone, indicating that he could work from it. "Thanks, Clara. I knew I could count on you."

Gloria didn't know why, but she'd just assumed that Owen would come, sit beside her the whole time, and be the buffer between her and, well, everyone. But he withdrew to the porch, and Gloria's heart thudded with each step of his retreat.

Chapter Six

Owen really did have emails to answer, but he also needed a minute. He couldn't help but feel like he'd fed Gloria to the lions. Their church had yet to pull off a musical without a disaster. At best, little Tommy emerged shirtless. At worst, the background came tumbling down. It had felt like a good idea when it first struck him, but now he felt like he might chuck.

Owen could almost hear Clara's deceased husband reminding him to breathe. His catch phrase was, *The good Lord didn't bring you this far just to abandon you, so don't you go abandoning Him.*

Clara's husband of forty-five years, Frank Brisbane, had been gone two years, having only lived for nine months after Owen accepted the call of lead pastor at Sycamore Hill Community Church. Frank faithfully mentored Owen for those nine months, meeting with him weekly to pray for the ministry and for him.

Frank encouraged Owen to be open and honest, and to resist stirrings of pride, which, according to Frank, made a man unwilling to hear constructive feedback or answer honest questions. Pride made a leader unapproachable and defensive and birthed an unhealthy focus on self. After the last pastor, the church needed a humble and approachable man at the helm of the ship.

Owen tried to imagine how Frank would counsel him right now. If they could sit on the porch's wicker furniture one more time, what would he say about Gloria? About the church? About the way Suzy and Janet were nosing about, certain they knew what Owen needed better than Owen did?

But to be fair, if Janet hadn't overheard Jillian at the restaurant, Owen might have never known of her grand scheme. He might have married the woman and been stuck for life on the hamster wheel of her insatiable ambition. He owed the church a debt of gratitude for saving him a lifetime of misery.

But he didn't owe them his life.

The thought came out of nowhere. Suddenly, Frank's wisdom, poured out over dozens and dozens of cups of coffee on this very porch, came rushing back.

Your vows are to God and your wife, not the church. A healthy marriage keeps Christ central, not ministry.

Sure, Frank thought his counsel would apply to Owen and Jillian, not Owen and Gloria, but it didn't make it any less right.

Trust the Lord to care for his church, and trust that He will care for you as you prioritize Him.

Owen wanted to emulate Clara and Frank's marriage. It thrived for forty-five years, keeping Christ central. That was what Owen wanted. Longevity in life, marriage, and ministry.

Lord, if You could put it on Clara's heart to be to Gloria what Frank was to me, I'd be so grateful. Owen eased his way across the porch, avoiding the creaky wooden slats, and claimed the rocker next to the window. He hadn't intended on listening. Not consciously. But just enough sound trickled out from inside the house to assure him the Lord answered his prayer.

"It's been two years since the good Lord took my Frank home," Mrs. Brisbane said to Gloria. "I thought it would get easier with time, but it hasn't."

"I'm sorry. I can't imagine the pain of such a loss." Gloria's reply was partially muffled by a clattering of ceramic dishes.

Owen's palms moistened at the clink of ceramic cups on saucers. The first time Clara had served Owen hot tea, he fumbled the tiny china like a monkey wearing mittens. Every visit since, she served his beverage in a fat mug, regardless of its contents.

"I saw the way Owen looked at you," Clara said. "The Lord is entrusting you with a great honor."

Owen peeked through the window.

Gloria's forehead crinkled. "How so?"

"The Lord's assigned this ministry to Owen. If I read

things right, by extension, that ministry is also being entrusted to you."

Gloria shook her head, loosening her hair so it fell forward and covered her profile. "Owen and I are not even engaged."

"Yet." Clara smiled in that way that drove Owen mad. It was the smile of a mom who knew which child stole the cookies despite posing the question. It was the smile of experience and indulgence. "There are good people here. This is a good church. It's not perfect, but it's good. You'll do just fine."

Clara shifted, and Owen ducked, his heart throbbing. He opened his email on his phone. *Focus!*

But the scraping sound of tissues being pulled from a box made Owen's heart skip. Was Gloria crying?

"I don't know if I'll make it." Her stifled words nearly flattened Owen.

Clara made motherly, supportive noises. "I understand you're applying for a job at the preschool. You've worked in a preschool before, haven't you?"

Owen dared another peek.

Gloria nodded and accepted a tissue from Clara. "But I am not applying for the job of Owen's wife. This is not something the church gets to vote on"—her voice dipped—"is it?"

Owen didn't hear much after that. Gloria wasn't applying for the job of his wife. The minute those words hit his ears, a roar filled his head. Each breath in hurt and each breath out sent pain to every nerve ending in his body.

Frank had warned Owen that ministry wives were sponges. They absorbed hit after hit over things like personal style, employment choices, and their involvement in the ministry. And every sponge has a saturation point. It's a point where it can absorb no more. But Owen couldn't believe it would happen here. Not to Gloria. Not even before they were married.

"Tiffany ruined my reputation in college." The resoluteness in Gloria's tone caught his ear. "I've been fighting all year to bring the truth to the light. The last thing I need is someone new dragging what's left of my name through the mud." A whimper escaped with her last word, and her intonation went from indignant to defeated.

"Oh honey, you have nothing to be ashamed of. I've followed the Emergence trial in the news. From what I can tell, speaking up took a lot of courage. The town should be grateful."

"Then why do I feel so ashamed?"

Owen's insides hardened. Gloria was the hero in the Emergence scandal.

"There was a time when shame didn't exist on earth," Clara said. "It was back in the garden. Adam and Eve were naked, and they were not ashamed."

Gloria snorted. "How does that help me now?"

"It shows us that when God makes right all that is

wrong in this world, one of the things He'll eradicate is shame."

"What do I do until then?"

"You remember your God. He didn't just take away your sin, He gave you His holiness. That's what defines you."

Owen practically *amened* before he remembered he was eavesdropping.

"Now." Clara's tone changed to all business. "About your need for a reference. I've been praying for someone to take the musical off my hands."

"You can hear better if you tip your head to the side."

Owen's entire body jerked, and he found himself eyeball to eyeball with Breanna Clarke. The rims of Owen's ears burned hot, and he pulled at the collar of his shirt. Busted.

Breanna's features perked, and she pressed her ear against the exterior siding and tilted her head. "Like this," she whispered, overly exaggerating a head tilt. Her eyebrows puckered. "Who we listening to?"

"Shouldn't you be in school?" Nice redirect, *Pastor*.

A chair scraped across the hardwood in the house. It took all of Owen's self-control to remain focused on Breanna and not peek into the house.

Breanna wrinkled her nose. "I'm going. Dad sent me to the drug store to pick up some milk. I just dropped it off."

"Afternoon, Pastor."

Owen's head whipped toward the sidewalk so fast he

tweaked a muscle. "Hey, Eli." Was the entire town taking the day off responsible work and school attendance?

"Nice day, isn't it?" One of Eli's eyebrows lifted with his real, unasked question.

Owen looked from Breanna, still listening through the wall, and back to Eli. They did make an odd pair.

"Yes, yes, it is." Owen straightened.

Owen's shoes slapped the stair boards loudly as he descended. Should he extend his hand? Fist bump? Do the one-armed hug with a double back slap? What was the proper greeting between men after getting caught eavesdropping? He went with stuffing both hands in his front pockets and hunching his shoulders. "How are the wedding plans coming along?"

"Great." Eli's gaze flicked momentarily to Meg's house, which stood next door to Clara's. "Meg has it all organized."

Eli and Meg didn't have a typical courtship by far, but Owen couldn't deny they were great together. He knew them as friends, but since he'd begun working through pre-marital counselling with them, he'd also found them to be solid, mature believers, committed to the Lord and each other. And even more, the four of them, Gloria, Owen, Meg, and Eli, really got on well together. What more could a man ask for? Owen glanced at Mrs. Brisbane's front door.

Approval from the masses?

"How are things with Gloria?" Eli probably knew

59

Owen better than anyone else in town. They met weekly for Bible study and accountability.

"Good. Things are good."

Breanna, still with her ear pressed against the wall, gave him a thumbs up. Owen winced. What was that rhyme Gloria was always spouting? *I've not seen a mess that I cannot wrangle, 'till I met this web that I cannot untangle!*

It was a mess, all right. As evidenced by the truant girl with her ear pressed to the wall.

The front door opened, and Clara saw him immediately.

And then Breanna.

And finally, Eli.

Like an experienced mother, she created a hierarchy of importance in a millisecond with minimal information and clucked her tongue. "What are you doing here during school hours, young lady?"

Mrs. Brisbane didn't need to speak twice. Breanna leapt from the porch to her scooter, lifting it from where she had dropped it in the grass and swinging it under her feet in one smooth motion. "See ya later, Pastor Owen!"

The seasoned woman turned her perceptive gaze to Owen, who instinctively ran a hand down the front of his shirt and smoothed his hair. "I thought you had emails to answer, Pastor?" Mrs. Brisbane raised her eyebrows until they disappeared under her hair. Even Eli straightened at her tone.

Owen's flesh prickled under a cold sweat. What was it

about Clara that made him revert to boyhood insecurities? He restuffed his hands in his pockets and clamped his elbows to his side. "I was, but then Eli and I got chatting."

"Ah, I better go. Meg's waiting for me." Eli scampered away.

Chicken.

"Thanks again, Clara. I can't tell you how much this visit has meant to me."

Mrs. Brisbane's steely gaze softened as it landed on Gloria. "Come again. We'll visit longer next time."

Owen laced his fingers with Gloria's, and they started back to the church. The way her lower lip continued to tremble birthed an ache in his bones. It was a whole-body ache like the kind that accompanied the flu.

Owen stopped walking. It was so sudden that Gloria stumbled a bit. He steadied her and then reached to tip Gloria's chin with his fingers, waiting until she met his eyes. The minute their gazes collided, her eyes filled with tears. He didn't care who might see them. He didn't care if he spent the rest of the day answering phone calls about an inappropriate public display of affection. All he cared about was the hurting woman standing in front of him. He'd seen the same vulnerability in her gaze when they were young, back when he'd naively believed that his certainty of her innocence would be enough. But only the Lord could fill the voids inside of her.

He swayed closer until only inches separated them. He tipped his head forward, and their foreheads touched.

"I'm sorry this hasn't gone the way you thought it would. I want you to know that I see your sacrifices. I see everything you are doing for us and for others. It makes me love you even more." Why had he waited so long to acknowledge her efforts?

Her eyes drifted shut. A single tear rolled down her cheek. "It's so much harder than I thought it would be."

Frank's warning returned. How much hurt could one person absorb?

Chapter Seven

S
o far, so good.

The morning was going well. *She* was doing well. Gloria had made it through introductions, smiling and nodding until she felt like her face would crack. This was harder than taking the stand in court to testify. Her insides flipped as she walked down the aisle to take her seat in the family pew. Like the eyes of the jurors interpreting her every hand gesture and facial expression, the congregation followed her movements. They released a collective sigh of approval when she joined the rest of the Sycamores. Owen had invited her to sit with him in the front of the church, but she kiboshed that idea before he'd even finished extending the invitation.

Gloria didn't actually breathe until she slid into the pew beside her family a few seconds before the first song, but that could have less to do with anxiety and more to do with how tightly her dress nipped in at her waist.

Her older sister, Jessica, scooched over to make room for Gloria beside her and her husband, Tate.

Emma and Meg snickered from the other side of the room, probably whispering about Gloria's crazy expectations for this morning.

Perfect. It was perfect. It is perfect. It will be perfect.

No pressure.

"What are you wearing?" Jessica whispered from the side of her mouth.

"Shhh," Gloria hissed. She straightened the skirt of her very conservative, beige, button-down-the-back dress that she bought yesterday from a clearance rack in the city. It felt a big snug in some spots, but the way the fabric gathered and draped hid that flaw well. A morning with an uncomfortable cinch at her waist was worth it to dress exactly how she imagined an acceptable pastor's wife would. Simple. Colorless. Boring.

Jessica's mouth puckered in the same way that Emma's had when Gloria had shown her the dress. "I don't think I've ever seen you in that color."

Was beige even a color? Wasn't it more of an absence of color?

"I'm trying to blend in." Which would work a lot better if Jessica stopped talking to her.

"With what? The walls?" Jessica stood as Owen invited the congregation to join him in song.

Gloria pushed to her feet only a half beat after everyone else. She'd already blown her first impression with Suzy and Janet; she was not blowing her chance with the entire congregation. Sure, they already knew her. But that was as the Sycamores' youngest child, the one that left school under a cloud of suspicion and scandal. Now she was Gloria Sycamore, the pastor's girlfriend and potential future wife. It changed the rules.

Gloria spent the last few days looking for a way to regain some sense of control over her move back home. Hitting those wrong notes with two key women was her fault. If she hadn't been so bold in her clothing choices, so made-up in cosmetics and hair, so certain that Owen should give her a reference, they might have seen her differently. So, from now on, she was playing it safe. Neutral. Flat. Opinionless.

She raised her eyes to the stained-glass window. *Help me, Lord*. Gloria tracked a water droplet building in size on the ceiling joist. It burst free and landed right on the microphone with an amplified splat. A wild storm had ripped through the community last night and peeled a few more shingles off the church. Owen ignored the intrusion and continued. Her chest swelled. What a pro.

The service moved along quickly. Owen's faithful proclamation from the Word made him even more irresistible to her. As she stole a glance around the room, an inner warmth intensified. Finding the pastor attractive had to be some sort of sin.

He wrapped up his message, and the tension inside her inflamed but for an entirely different reason. She didn't hear a word of Owen's final prayer. Instead, she mapped out her exit. So far, nothing outright disastrous had occurred. She just had to get out with her dignity intact.

"Amen."

Gloria eyes snapped open. *It's go time.*

"I'll see you at home," she whispered to Jessica. Gloria wiggled out of the pew and hightailed it to the back door. Ten feet. She smiled wildly. Six feet. Her cheeks hurt. Three feet.

"Gloria!"

Busted.

A family brushed past her and exited out the front double doors, giving her a glimpse of the parking lot before they swung shut again. So close.

Gloria forced a big smile as she turned. "Happy Sunday."

"Yes, yes." The woman flapped her hands as if she had no time for pleasantries. She leaned in, and with a colluding tone, whispered, "I'm Nettie Fry, and the first thing you need to know about me is that I'm not one for gossip, so when *someone*, and I won't say who, because I'm not a gossip, started flapping her gums, I said, 'Hold up. I won't have any part of that. I'm just going to ask her myself.'"

Gloria gulped. The back door might as well be a million miles away.

"What's this I hear about you and Pastor Owen at the hotel in the city? We can't have our pastor at the center of a scandal."

Pressure rushed to Gloria's head at the same time

the muscles in her body slackened. Had Suzy said something to this Nettie woman? And after Owen clarified everything? Gloria opened her mouth, but before a word came out, she felt a popping up her back. It rippled from her waist all the way to the nape of her neck like a row of dominos falling. Coolness hit her spine.

Gloria clutched at the back of her dress as the fabric around her hips sprung free and moved up toward the waistline. She backed away from Nettie. With each step, she felt a bit more of the fabric give. She didn't dare turn around. She retreated toward the side hall that led into the restrooms. *Please, Lord, let the hallway be empty!*

Gloria burst into the restroom and crashed into the furthest stall as the entire back of her dress gave way. This was it. This was how she was going to die.

Gloria slammed the stall door closed and twisted the lock. She pressed her forehead against the back of it. She should have never let her insecurities get to her. She should have worn an old favorite outfit, a tried-and-true combo that made her feel like a million bucks. Instead, she let all the comments about Jillian mess with her, prompting her to spend money she didn't have on a dress that malfunctioned *at church!*

A cool breeze tickled her back end. Her *exposed* back end. Her dress had split from top to bottom.

She twisted at the waist to try and see if any buttons remained. She yanked on edges. If it would just wrap around her . . . Did skin swell under stress? Maybe her anxiety about this morning caused her to retain water. There just wasn't enough fabric to cover her body.

"Gloria, are you okay?" Owen called through the outer restroom door. "Mrs. Fry said you'd rushed off."

Ha! That was putting it mildly. "I'm fine," she called out in a too-cheery voice. "Be out in a minute."

She slipped her arms out of the dress to assess the damage. She must have left a trail of buttons from the foyer to the restroom, because not a single one remained. She put the dress on backward and tried to wrap it around herself. No luck. She couldn't very well waltz out of the church with the front of her dress open with only her bra and granny panties underneath.

She wasn't sure if her constricted lungs were from the seemingly ever-shrinking bathroom stall or the onset of a panic attack. Her breaths came harder and faster. She couldn't breathe. No, that wasn't right. She *was* breathing. Panting, actually. Like a racehorse after a win.

Calm down. Nobody knows. You're in here alone. Just leave the stall, go into the sink, and use the mirror to figure out how to cover yourself.

She gulped. She pressed both palms against the door. *But what if somebody came in?* She flashed back to elementary school. She had hidden in a restroom stall while her best friend asked the popular kids what they *really* thought of Gloria Sycamore. She should have known better. Eavesdroppers never heard kind words. But she had hoped—had longed—to hear they admired her. Liked her. Wanted to be her friend. Instead, Gloria perched on the toilet seat with her knees pulled into her chest and buried her face. Never-good-enough Gloria. Geeky Gloria.

Her hands grappled for anything fabric to hold onto, and she heaved on the dress again. If she could just stretch the material— She couldn't leave the safety of the stall. She couldn't.

Her heart throbbed. The heat from her body must have made the dress shrink. She couldn't cover herself. It was some sort of malfunctioning fabric, and that was why it had been on sale.

She contorted her limbs like an acrobat, trying everything to force the fabric to cover the most intimate parts of her body. But however she twisted, something hung out.

"Gloria?" Owen rapped on the door.

"In a minute," she repeated.

What exactly was she going to do in a minute? Waltz through the church half naked? Nope. Call Owen in to help? That wasn't an option. Her mother? *Her mother!*

"Owen," she called sweetly, "Could you grab my mom for me? I need a hand."

"Sure." His footsteps faded.

Now, if only no one else entered the restroom. *God, if you can hear me, please—*

The outer door burst open, and giggling girls bounded in.

Forget it.

"Breanna banana." More giggling was followed by what sounded like a little bit of shoving.

"Leave me alone."

"Breanna banana wears smelly pajamas."

Pajamas. The school must have had a P.J. day on Friday. That's why she was dressed in them.

"Get lost," Breanna growled.

The high-pitched laugher of preadolescent girls mixed with quiet sniffs.

"What's going on out there?" Gloria used her sternest teacher-voice.

Silence.

Dead air.

A pregnant pause.

There was one more loud sniff, and the sound of the door opening and closing again, and more footsteps. Had someone planned a party in the restroom after church? For crying out loud, there were more people gathering here than in the church foyer.

"Gloria?" Her mother called. "Are you in here? I thought you'd gone home."

The tears that pooled in Gloria's eyes were second in volume to the moisture that pooled under her armpits. "In here," she hissed.

"Where?" Her mother's heels clicked as they tapped the floor.

"The last stall. Help."

The girls giggled some more. A few hushed, unintelligible words, then more giggles. Then the door swooshing open and closed.

Silence.

Gloria cracked the stall door. "My dress ripped."

Her mom's chuckles were not helping. Gloria opened the stall door completely and folded her arms around her middle. "The buttons are somewhere in the foyer."

"Oh, dear." Mom pressed a hand to her mouth.

The bathroom stall blurred in and out of focus. She was going to die in the Sycamore Hill Community Church restroom. Those girls would be telling this story at youth retreats for years to come. No one would remember her name; she would be the crazy woman who thought she'd marry the pastor but met her Maker after being bested by a faulty dress. *An ugly, faulty dress.* The kind of dress Gloria would have never bought had she not already been feeling insecure. The story embellishments would make her a legend. She'd have to leave town again, and this time, she'd never come back.

"Can you wrap it around like a housecoat?" Mom tugged on the material.

Tears squirted from Gloria's eyes. "I tried."

"I know! I'll get my jacket. It's long enough to cover you. Don't go anywhere." Her mother winked and hurried off.

Gloria couldn't bear another minute stuck in this stall, stuck in this bathroom, stuck in this church, in this humiliation. But where was she going to go? She backed into the tiny cubicle and closed it again, twisting the lock for good measure. She perched on the toilet seat and gnawed on a fingernail. This was not how today was supposed to play out. Today, she'd planned to win over Owen's congregation. She was going to prove to them that she belonged at his side, in this church, and in the community. But she'd only been here one Sunday, and she was already a cautionary tale.

The door opened again. Gloria shot to her feet. "Mo—"

"Can you believe it? She just up and left me. Mid-sentence. I was hopeful, but now I'm not so sure about that girl."

Gloria recognized Nettie's voice. *Oh God, I know I haven't prayed as much as I should. But please, please, please, let me get out of here without them seeing me.*

"I saw them myself, sneaking out of that hotel in the city. A hotel!"

It had to be Suzy.

"We can't let our pastor be taken in," Suzy continued. "He'll come to his senses and see that the type of woman he needs by his side is *not* Gloria Sycamore."

It was the elementary school humiliation all over again.

"I read an article in the paper that said they might discount her testimony at the trial because she's . . ."

Gloria stiffened and knocked the garbage container. Conversation stopped. *She's what? Why didn't the woman finish her sentence? Was she spinning her index finger near the temple, implying Gloria was mentally unstable?*

Disbelief shot through her until she looked down at her dress gaping like a poorly tied hospital gown. She returned to her perch on the toilet in the church bathroom with her feet pulled up. Not exactly the actions of a sane woman.

"Someone needs to speak with Pastor Owen. Dating a parishioner is like a doctor dating a patient. It's just wrong."

Gloria nearly snorted. These two gossips were going to talk about ethics? She should just waltz out there and join the conversation. That would cork their mouths.

And prove she was no longer the same insecure girl she once was.

"It's like a professor dating a student."

"It does seem to be an imbalanced relationship."

"Imbalanced is right. I never pegged Pastor Owen as the controlling type, but this makes me wonder about his character. What do we really know about him? Who dates a person they have authority over unless they like control?"

"I got my jacke—" Gloria's mom clipped her words short. Her strides shortened as if she'd skidded to a stop. "Oh, sorry. I didn't know anyone else was in here. Gloria, are you still here?"

Like she'd be anywhere else.

"Gloria's here?" Their voices hit the same notes as the preteen bullies.

Good. They should feel bad. Still, the pressure that pinched Gloria's chest was worse than the dress. What if they were right? What if her presence brought more harm to Owen's ministry than good? She squeezed her eyes closed. *Lord, if you're ever coming back for your people, now would be a good time.*

She waited.

She cracked open one eye.

Nothing.

She swallowed. "I'm back here, Mom."

The gossip girls inhaled audibly and exited without another word.

Gloria opened the door. *Just when you think it's the worst it can get, your problems grow troubles and worsen with fret.*

Her mom held out her jacket. "Can you put this over it?"

Gloria slipped her arms through the jacket sleeves. Her mom stood in front of her and buttoned the jacket like a mother dressing her toddler. "Come on, love," she gently prodded. "You need to laugh. It's laugh or cry."

Gloria sucked her bottom lip into her mouth and bit down hard enough to draw blood. She was not going to cry. If she did, she'd have to face the congregation not only as a streaker in a trench coat but also with the blotchy skin that came from bawling.

Gloria lifted her chin and forced her stiff face into a plastic smile quickly becoming all too familiar.

Chapter Eight

Owen looked at his watch for what felt like the millionth time. How long did it take to put on a new dress? The church doors yawned open behind him, providing people with easy access to second helpings of food. Two long tables positioned end-to-end filled the church lobby, and the rest of the party had spilled outside despite the crisp fall day.

"Gloria will be back soon," Owen repeated to Nettie for what felt like the millionth time. After Gloria's disappearing act following the service, he'd been fielding questions about her from everyone. He'd done what he could to deflect from her clothing mishap, but word spread. His girl had a cringe-worthy wardrobe malfunction in the back of the church sanctuary.

Fantastic.

Owen smiled and waved at several people. He stuffed his hands into his pant pockets and tried to focus on

Nettie, still talking away at him. Talking at him, not with him, because that was the way it usually was. In the crowd but not part of the crowd. Participating in the conversation as a listener, not a contributor.

Off to the right, Hank Sinclair bent down on one knee and was showing Tommy how to properly fold a paper airplane from the papers they handed out for sermon notes. Eli and Meg chatted with Kathryn and Ethan. Meg worked at Ethan's bakery, and she'd brought some of his famous muffins to the potluck. They were the first to go. Kim Jansen gripped her son's hand as Oliver tried to pull her toward the buffet table for what would be his third helping. Officer Jackson, Oliver's uncle, picked the boy up and swung him around like he was weightless, which, at less than three years old, he practically was, despite his robust appetite.

Nettie flapped her hands like a concerned mother hen ruffling her feathers and clucked to regain Owen's attention. She actually clucked, and Owen had to clamp his teeth together to hold back a laugh.

"Oh, Pastor, it was awful, just awful. You don't know what it is like to be a woman and have something like that happen. Her dress ripped." She leaned in, hushed. "And at church!"

True. He didn't know. But to be fair, neither did Nettie. And for all her showy compassion, Nettie was the one standing here still talking about it.

"She must be devastated. Humiliated. I'm mean, to show your"—Nettie lowered her voice— "backside—"

"I think I'm needed in the . . . the . . ." He didn't have an end to that sentence. He simply needed to stop the conversation. He headed for the buffet table under the guise of a second helping. Dozens of empty casserole dishes, serving spoons, and ladles were scattered across the surface. Picked-over leftovers and Gloria's contribution were all that remained. A white, square, ceramic tray filled with hand-rolled cucumber sushi sat mostly untouched beside a cup of single-use chopsticks that Gloria insisted the kids would enjoy. He'd been the only person to take some. Owen piled four more tightly-rolled seaweed and rice discs onto his plate.

"Are we still on for this week?" Eli perused the leftovers. At Owen's blank look, he added, "For pre-marriage counselling."

Right. Owen clicked his chopsticks. "Yes, we'll discuss chapter four in our book." As Owen reminded Eli of his assigned reading on becoming the kind of husband Meg needed, he realized that he'd failed to apply the material to himself personally. It wasn't enough for Gloria to know that he loved God; she needed to know that he loved her. The church could always get another pastor if things went south, but Gloria couldn't get another husband after they married.

If they married.

Technically, they weren't even engaged. But that wasn't the point. The point was that if he planned to marry her, he needed to start acting like the man God had called him to be.

"There you are!" As Clara Brisbane hustled toward him, Eli wandered away. "Is Gloria okay?"

"I haven't seen her since she left. Hopefully, she'll be back soon." They chatted a bit longer before parting ways. Before another person could descend, Owen slid into the corridor outside his office. He leaned against the wall, tipped his head back, and closed his eyes.

"Pastor?"

His eyes snapped open.

Suzy sat at Janet's desk just outside his office door. She folded her hands over her swollen belly and smiled up from her seat. "Are you all right?"

Owen couldn't remember the last time he walked around a corner and Suzy wasn't there.

"I was just going to check my calendar. I can't remember if I have a meeting Monday afternoon or not."

"Oh, let me do that for you." Suzy opened the shared calendar on the desktop. "Schedule's all clear. Would you like me to insert something?"

What he'd like is to know what Suzy was doing at the desk opening the church calendar as if she was the church secretary, but his mental exhaustion wouldn't let him pull on that thread.

"I'm going to pop into the musical practice. Can you block off a few hours, please?"

His breath bottled as he waited for Suzy's typical nosy follow-up question, but it never came.

"All done."

"Thanks." Owen didn't want to return to the

potluck and socialize. He couldn't hide in his office with Suzy just outside the door, so he retreated to the sanctuary. He slipped into the back pew and cradled his head in his hands. *Lord, help Gloria find her footing here. Help me help her.*

He felt her presence beside him.

"Did anyone notice?" Gloria's attention alternated between Owen and the exterior doors. On the other side of the open doors, small clusters of people milled about with coffee and baked goods. The occasional shriek of pleasure from one of the kids cut through the crisp air.

"Yes, they noticed, but I covered for you." At least he hoped he did.

He knew the moment her gaze landed on the buffet table, which was just visible from their position. She sagged, features, countenance, and body. She tried so hard. Why couldn't the church just embrace her? Or at the very least, indulge her.

"The sushi was a flop?" She meandered toward the foyer.

He caught up to her in two short strides.

She dragged a fingertip along the edge of the large square platter holding her offering. The muscles in her jaw clenched and released. With a fire he'd never felt before, Owen's insides burned. He wanted to take it all away. The disappointment. The rejection. The judgment. But he couldn't. Those feelings were intrinsically connected to ministry. To all of life.

A profound disappointment in his people settled

over his heart. God had called him to serve these people. They were an imperfect lot that needed the Lord just as much as anybody else. The expectation or hope that they'd function differently was both right and wrong. As born-again believers, they should live differently. They should be filled with love, joy, peace, patience, kindness, goodness, gentleness, faithfulness, and self-control. But they were still people wrapped in sinful flesh that sometimes responded to circumstances with hate, sorrow, disruption, impatience, hurt, sinfulness, abrasiveness, unfaithfulness, and impatience. Sanctification was a journey. Yet, however they may have disappointed him, they were still blood-bought children of God, and therefore deserved his tender affection. He and they were sinners that struggled with sin, and that was normal.

But it didn't feel good.

And it didn't feel normal or right for Gloria to absorb the hits.

"I had the sushi." He lifted his plate. "It was great. I'm on seconds."

Her lips tipped up in a tiny, sad smile.

Owen had never eaten sushi before meeting Gloria. He'd wrongly assumed it was always filled with raw fish. Turned out there were several kinds of sushi. Avocado. Cucumber. Sweet potato. It had quickly become a favorite treat, but he couldn't convince anyone else to try it.

When Gloria lifted her head, her expression of defeat stole his breath. "What are we doing?"

The muscle in his cheek began to twitch. He didn't like her tone or the look in her eyes. It reminded him of a younger Gloria, freshly accused of cheating and expelled from school. "We're having lunch."

She wrapped her arms around her middle and hugged herself. If half the town wasn't watching, Owen would have folded his arms around her and kissed away her sadness.

But they were.

So, he didn't.

"Us." She gestured between them. "What are we doing? I'll never fit in. They'll never accept me." She blinked rapidly, and when they made eye contact, she quickly looked away.

"Don't say that." Owen pressed a finger against her lips. "They'll love you when they get to know you."

Gloria snorted. Her gaze trailed longingly over the crowd. Owen followed the path her eyes took. Groups of women laughed together. Children ran. Despite all the questions he had fielded about Gloria, no one approached her to invite her in. Outside of her family, Meg, and Emma, Gloria was pretty much left on her own. The church should be a safe space where everyone felt welcome, but too often it functioned like a social club. "Give them time."

"There is not enough time in the world."

"Are you ready for tomorrow, dear?" Mrs. Brisbane hurried over. She looked Gloria up and down. "I see you've changed your clothes."

Owen stiffened, but before he could speak, Clara continued with a wave of her hands. "This suits you much better than that old frock that ripped," she tutted. "You're far too young for that fuddy-duddy style."

Owen's mouth fell open. Had he not been shocked into silence, he would have let out a wallop of a cheer. Thank the Lord for Clara Brisbane.

"Are you ready?" Clara repeated her question and cocked an eyebrow so high it tucked itself under the log curl on her forehead.

Gloria blinked but remained silent.

"The musical? Have you got everything you need? I told the children that your rehearsals start tomorrow."

"Right, right, the musical." Gloria smiled. This was a real smile. Not the kind she pasted on earlier as she mingled with parishioners. Not the frightened one she wore as she escaped wrapped in a jacket. But a real one. The kind that only emerged when she spoke about her kids, as she called them. "I love the play. Where did you find it?" Gloria turned to Owen. "It's called Buzz Off. It's super cute. It's all about bees."

Mrs. Brisbane patted Gloria's hand. "I can't wait to see what you do with those kids. You have complete freedom to take it in whatever direction you want. I'm just so thankful for your help."

Complete freedom. That could be good.

Or, if the church community continued to resist her, very, very bad.

Chapter Nine

The church multipurpose room smelled more than a little damp, but it was the scent of wiggly bodies that triggered some sort of dopamine release in Gloria. Like a timed-release shot of maternal instinct, her biological clock kicked into high gear. She couldn't get enough. About twenty children of various ages clamored around her, and she hadn't felt this good—this needed—since her last day in the preschool.

"Who is excited about our play?" Gloria sat down on a chair and motioned for the kids to follow suit. She kept her voice low, refusing to raise it above the chatter. Experience had already taught her the value of a soft word. Proverbs 15:1 not only defused an angry child effectively, but noisy ones as well.

Quiet rolled over the room, and the kids dropped to their bottoms.

Clara Brisbane's head nod injected a shot of confidence into Gloria. She could do this. She would do this. If she wanted any chance of scoring that job and staying in Sycamore Hill, she not only had to do this, but she had to do it well.

Instead of nervousness, excitement powered her pulse. It was the same kind of feverish thrill that hit her parents' dog when guests arrived and made him leave a puddle on the floor. It was the perfect case of I-can't-hold-back-the-wiggles kind of eagerness, but-I-have-to-because-I'm-the-teacher dilemma. Gloria stretched her eyes as wide as she could, playing up the moment. She leaned forward, sitting on the edge of her chair as if she were about to share the most delicious secret. "Our play is called Buzz Off. You've all been working on it for weeks, but I've just learned about it. Can someone tell me what the play is about?"

Silence.

"Is it," Gloria tapped a fingertip to her lips, "an angry big sister telling her brother to," she mouthed the words *buzz off*.

A child in the front row giggled.

"Is it about a bully?"

"No," a younger voice called out.

"Is it about someone who is mean?"

Laughter peppered out from the kids.

"Hmmmm. Such a puzzle."

"The main characters are *bees*," a preadolescent voice called from the back row. It sounded slightly bored with Gloria's game.

"Like bumble bees? Honeybees?"

"I don't like bees." One of the smallest in the group pulled back so far that he was almost sitting in the lap of the kid behind him. He popped his thumb into his mouth and started twirling a chunk of hair that was about four weeks late for a haircut. His twin sister, Bethann, slung an arm around his shoulder, looking every bit the part of a fierce defender.

Gloria melted. "It's Brock, right?"

He nodded.

"Bees are in the story, but it's also about two boys. Can you tell me about the boys?"

Brock looked to his sister for insight despite the fact she could only be older than him by mere minutes. The girl nodded. It was a curt, tight nod that told Gloria the poor thing had done far more mothering than any four-year-old should ever have to do.

Nathan's twins.

Even if Clara hadn't pointed them out when they arrived, Gloria would have guessed. All four siblings had the same heart-shaped face and wild, brown hair. It sprung in all directions, but the twins' hair retained the downy softness of babyhood.

Clara tapped a few pre-teens on the shoulder and slipped out the back door with them as the rest of the children waited on Gloria. Clara was working with the actors, running lines and reviewing stage direction. Gloria had the daunting task of managing the choir. A dozen kids of various ages on risers, instructed to stand still, be quiet, and not fidget. Possible? Of course. Fun? Hardly.

That was all about to change because she had *complete freedom*.

Clara had given Gloria the run-down of how she usually taught the kids their songs. Those who could read were given the lyrics, and those that couldn't, listened as they sang the songs over and over. This was how it had been done for years. Decades. *Centuries,* maybe. Clara didn't buy into the new student-driven, need-based theories in education. What she'd been doing for years had worked just fine. It wasn't broke, so there was no need to fix it.

That might have been true, but it didn't mean they couldn't improve upon it. Gloria pulled from the students a summary of the musical, outlining the roles of two boys struggling to get along, the bee colony facing division, and the theme of forgiveness. She wanted to hear what part of the story resonated with the kids and got them excited. She followed along in the script Clara had pressed into her hands. "So, the worker bees are trying to run out the drones, who, according to them, don't contribute anything to the colony. Is that right?"

Luke shoved Breanna. "Sounds like you. Useless."

Breanna stomped on her brother's foot. Hard.

There was a gigantic pause like those few moments of calm before a storm ripped through the neighborhood and tore roofs off houses. Luke sucked in a breath—the kind you take before plunging into the lake— and then, he howled. Not just any kind of howl. He howled like a caged dog. He clasped one foot in his hands and hopped on the other, glaring at his sister with such loathing that if looks could kill, Breanna would be face to face with her Maker.

Brian and Sarah, whose gaga eyes for each other hadn't escaped Gloria's attention, used the distraction to drift to the back of the group and erase the space between them like a north magnetic pole finding the south.

"Oh, no you don't." Gloria wagged her finger at the pair who were not-quite-old-enough-to-be-a-couple but plenty old-enough-to-feel-the-early-pangs-of-attraction.

Bethann's finger found Brock's ear, which she poked in, withdrew, examined, and then popped in her mouth.

Gloria gagged.

This was a million times worse than her preschoolers. Wasn't it supposed to get easier as children aged? Shouldn't they be more responsible? What would Clara think—

And it hit her.

It hit her like a baseball bat to the gut. The kind of impact that forces the breath from your body and leaves you gasping.

Clara knew.

She *knew* these kids. She'd run the musical for years. Years! This wasn't a test run for Gloria's referral. This was flat-out sabotage.

Gloria swiveled to the back of the room and stared at the door through which Clara and her handpicked students had vanished. She was probably on the other side drumming her fingertips together in front of her face and barely holding back maniacal laughter. She'd set Gloria up to fail.

Not if Gloria had anything to say about it. "Everybody up."

The kids jolted at her abrupt shift in tone and stood. In her periphery, she caught a flicker of surprise in Breanna's eyes. Maybe even a twinge of respect. If the kids expected a pushover, they had another thing coming.

"Get into a line right here." Gloria extended her hand in front of her. When nobody moved, she scooped up Bethann, swung her around, and deposited her first in line. "Behind Bethann, please."

They fell into a messy row that her preschoolers could have put to shame.

"Worker bees are hardly ever still, so I think," Gloria cupped one elbow with her hand and twisted her lips. She circled the kids slowly. "This choir needs to move."

"We aren't allowed to move," Luke piped up.

"We haffa stay still." Brock spoke around two slobbery fingers. Bethann's head bobbed generously. They were the youngest in the crew—only four years old. Old enough to know how the annual musical played out.

Quiet.

Still.

No fun.

But Gloria had too much riding on this musical to bank on Clara's word that her instructions were best.

Sitting still clearly wasn't working for the squirmy litter. Some adults might see their energy as a weakness, but Gloria would make it a strength.

"I get to decide how the musical part of the play works, and I think that we are going to need"—she tapped her lips for a few more beats— "two ribbon dancers and a ballet dancer."

A few of the girls in the back perked up. Sarah actually ripped her eyes off Brian for a few seconds.

"I see a conga line and, of course, we need the usual choir. We don't want to disappoint our parents who are looking forward to that. But this choir will not stand still or be quiet. This choir will dance." Gloria swayed with exaggerated movements. "It needs to dance. And costumes!" She clapped her hands. "We'll need lots of costumes."

Her declarations landed like pebbles in the water that rippled joy across the faces of the children.

"We never get costumes."

"This'll be fun."

"I hope I get picked for ballet."

Only Breanna remained quiet.

"Why don't we spend the rest of our time making flower masks? The opening song happens in a garden, so we should all look like flowers."

Happy chatter and fresh energy soon pushed out the negative vibes. Gloria pulled craft supplies from the large cabinet at the back of the room and showed the kids how to make a simple flower mask with construction paper, a paper plate, and a popsicle stick. "We need it on a stick so we can pull it down when we are singing and put the mask back up when we are done."

As the kids worked, Gloria played the songs the choir would sing in the background. It wasn't too long before the humming started. Then, the occasional line would slip out while a child focused on their task. Gloria's chest puffed. There was more than one way to learn lyrics. She wandered up and down and around the tables until she stood behind Breanna, who leaned over her six-year-old brother, Luke, and rubbed paste on the end of a stick.

"Are you excited about the play?" Gloria asked her.

Breanna shrugged.

"Is something bothering you?"

Breanna darted a look at her brother, who was now happily drawing on a piece of paper. She stepped away from him. "Dad don't have extra money for costumes or ribbons."

Right then and there, Gloria made an executive decision. She hadn't asked Clara how the church managed extra expenses, but she didn't care. She'd pay out of pocket if she had to. "Don't you worry about that. We're making all the costumes ourselves right here at every practice."

"Really?" Breanna's eyes lightened briefly, but they still held the kind of doubt that came from experience. The kind that knew what it was to be promised one thing yet receive another.

"Really." Gloria squeezed her shoulder. "And it's

sweet of you to be concerned about your dad's money, but God always provides exactly what we need just when we need it, often in ways we cannot imagine."

The shadow of a smile started. Millimeter by millimeter it grew into a full-out grin. It took years off the girl. Gloria handed her a paper plate and glitter. "You better get to work."

Breanna trotted off.

"That was sweet."

Owen.

An unexpected shiver tiptoed down Gloria's spine. By the time she faced him, she was sure the same goofy grin that Breanna just sported was pasted on her face. And maybe Sarah's gaga eyes, to boot. "What are you doing here? Isn't Monday your day off?"

Owen's crinkly smile widened as his gaze moved over the busy kids. "I came to see how it was going. I thought you were supposed to be getting them ready to sing?"

"I am."

His eyebrows pulled together.

"Trust me." She reached for both his hands and squeezed them in hers. "They need this."

They stood there, smiling at each other for an uncomfortably long second. For a brief moment, she thought he might challenge her, until his features relaxed. "They look like they are having fun."

The kids threw them covert glances and giggled. Owen pulled his hands out of hers and put a more respectable amount of space between them.

Room for the Holy Spirit, her mother used to say.

"I also came in to check the donations that came in for the roof. After yesterday—well, we need to do something."

"The funds are here?"

"Yeah. The bookkeeper will deposit them later today. For now, they are in my office in a locked drawer. Some more came in yesterday's offering, so I want to see where we're at with it."

Gloria nodded.

"Do you have time for dinner tonight?"

"I can't. Meg, Emma, and I are working on Meg's wedding favors, and after that I have a phone call scheduled with the lawyer. He thinks I'll be called back to the stand for a redirect."

His voice dropped to a whisper and Gloria leaned in before realizing he'd pulled her quiet trick on her. "Do you think they'd notice if I kissed you goodbye?"

Her eyes bulged. The collar of her shirt suddenly felt tight. He was teasing. He had to be.

"Just kidding." He lightly squeezed her fingertips. "I only wanted to see you blush."

She glanced at the window and saw her reflection. Mission accomplished. Blotchy. Flustered. Beet red. Just how every girl wanted to look.

"You're gorgeous." His words dripped with intimacy that couldn't possibly be acceptable in a church. Wasn't the ground holy or something?

Breanna's lips curved, and Gloria's skin prickled even more.

"Until later." Owen's promise caressed her ear. He raised his head and called out, "Bye, kids!"

"Bye, Pastor Owen!"

Gloria distracted herself with opening up a large fabric grocery bag that she'd brought with her. "I think it's time for a treat!"

Hoots and hollers validated her decision.

Gloria removed boxes of pre-made food with no nuts, dairy, or gluten. It cost a fortune to buy everything pre-packaged, but better safe than sorry.

Tommy grabbed fistful of soft, red gummies. "I love these!" He shoved them into his mouth and raced around the table.

Of course, this was when Clara returned with her actors in tow. Her eyebrows disappeared into that sausage roll that forever sat across her forehead, and Gloria suddenly saw the organized chaos through the older woman's eyes.

Tommy had his shirt off and twirled it like a lasso above his head. The twins shrieked like they were having some sort of squawking contest. Luke bellowed out the lyrics of the song, one word behind and completely off key.

Gloria gulped.

So much for her recommendation.

Chapter Ten

A harsh knock on his office door jolted Owen from his sermon prep. Janet never let anyone interrupt him during this part of his week. "Come in."

Jason Chalkey entered and closed the door behind him. Not a good sign. "Morning, Owen."

"Hey, Jason, what can I do for you?" Owen gestured to the chair across from his desk. A million questions flashed through his mind, beginning with how Jason had broken through the gatekeeper and ending with why Jason had used his given name. The congregation had always addressed him as pastor. Not that he asked or wanted them to. They just did. Jason's reversal to his given name landed with a hint of disrespect and a passive-aggressive gut punch. "Did Suzy have the baby?"

Jason's neck corded. He worked his jaw back and forth and avoided direct eye contact.

Owen stiffened. Something had happened. Something bad. He fought to reel in his catastrophizing thoughts. Were there complications with Suzy's pregnancy? Did their house finally sink under sea level?

The Chalkey family's money struggles were well known. They'd bought a beautiful home in the country, large enough for their growing brood and well under market value. Then, they found out why the as-is deal that was too good to be true was, in fact, too good to be true. As winter turned to spring, the melting snow filled their basement with water. Every storm or hard rain refilled the space. This past fall, with the series of storms tracking through the area, had been particularly difficult. They'd taken to living on the main floor and blocking access to the basement. Losing half their living space had been difficult. The church was trying to help, but the projected price tag for the fix had come in at close to twenty thousand dollars. No one had that kind of cash, not when the church also needed a new roof. They were praying for a miracle.

"We need to have a discussion about the roof." Jason ignored the offered chair and remained standing, spreading his legs further apart and folding his arms across his chest.

Owen tapped his index finger on the desktop as a tiny release for his pent-up energy. He'd have to chat with Janet later. This was not an interrupt-sermon-prep-day sort of situation. He scrubbed his hand down his face and was just about to say that he didn't have time for this when Jason shifted like a linebacker preparing to pounce. "The money's gone."

Wait. What? Owen's insides momentarily hollowed. He briefly closed his eyes, trying to settle the big breakfast he'd eaten at The Muffin Man that now rolled dangerously through his midsection. "What do you mean gone?"

"Gone. Lost." Jason's nostrils flared. "Stolen."

"I counted the offering yesterday." Owen fumbled for the key to his locked desk drawer. Janet was the only other person who had a key. He shoved the key in, but it didn't unlatch anything. The drawer, already unlocked, opened easily. Busted, actually. "The money was here. All of it."

"Janet called me as soon as she arrived this morning and saw the broken lock." Jason rolled onto the balls of his feet and then back again. Back and forth. Over and over.

She saw the busted lock? What had she been doing in his office? How many times had she poked around in here without his knowledge? But he didn't ask any of those questions. He was too busy trying to remember if he'd ever left sensitive information from counselling sessions out on his desk.

"She called you?" Owen repeated Jason's statement. Why hadn't Janet called him? Why had she acted as if everything was fine when he said good morning to her and sat a coffee from the bakery on her desk?

Then it hit him. It hit him so hard that if he hadn't already been seated, he would have dropped.

They've been here before.

Jason blurred in and out of focus. Owen's tongue thickened, and his throat closed in. They thought he'd taken the money. To do what? Impress a girl already dating him? To splurge on a fancy meal in the city? But Jason's hard lines and stiff posture held no mercy.

Not because Owen wasn't trustworthy, but because the wounds the last guy inflicted were fresh and still bleeding.

"Some of the kids mentioned seeing you at music practice." Some of the kids. So, he'd already called parents. Checked his alibi. Owen stretched his neck on the chopping block and waited.

The ache started at the back of this throat. His chest tingled, and his fingertips went numb. Owen dropped his hands to his lap and clenched them away from Jason's accusingly hard stare.

"What were you doing at the church on your day off?" Jason's angled body and lowered head made Owen want to squirm.

He fought the urge.

Jason's brow wrinkled, and the longer Owen took to reply, the deeper Jason's skin flushed.

"I came to see Gloria." It came out whispery. Owen cleared his throat and tried again. He had nothing to apologize for, and this wasn't personal, no matter how personal it felt. Considering the church history, Jason had to ask these questions, and Owen had to put their minds at ease. "I also checked the fund while I was here. I've been investigating what it would cost to temporarily patch the roof. I wanted to see how much we had. The lock was intact then, so it had to happen in the evening or overnight."

But if it wasn't personal, if Jason standing here, asking these questions was the right next step, why was the room still spinning?

"Suzy said that you and Gloria have been eating in some pretty fancy places. Are the restaurants in Sycamore Hill not good enough?" Jason's arms tightened as if his hands needed to be tucked under his armpits to maintain control. "I'd love to take Suzy to Queens Court, but we have to settle for lunch at the diner."

Owen lifted his chin. That wasn't fair. Under normal circumstances, Owen wasn't obligated to explain how long he saved for that date or how many cans of soup he ate for dinner afterward, but these weren't normal circumstance. Still, he couldn't hide the hurt in his voice. "Stop beating around the bush and say your piece like a man."

Jason's noisy breath whistled through his nostrils. His eyes turned cold and flinty. "Have you dipped into the roof fund to impress Gloria?"

And there it was. All the years invested in this place gone in a single accusation. Shame descended on Owen with such oppressiveness that he couldn't inhale. Not shame over his actions, because he'd done nothing wrong, but shame nonetheless. Shame over what had been done to him. Assumed of him. Doubted in him. He felt *unclean*. Leviticus unclean.

Owen finally understood Gloria's struggles with the trial and people's endless questions because of her association with something tawdry. He felt that same contamination right now. Scripture devoted a whole bunch of Old Testament words to the subject of cleanliness and what it meant to be sent out from the camp.

But unclean was not the same as sinful.

Unclean can return to the community.

But was this the community they wanted to re-enter?

It might not even matter. There might not have been a way for Owen to recover from the accusation, but Owen wouldn't go down without a fight. He held Jason's gaze. "I did not take the money."

"It doesn't look good when the pastor lives a flashy life. Image matters. We're simple people. Most barely getting by."

Flashy? Owen lived in a one-bedroom apartment in the attic of a small house off Main Street. He ate ramen noodles and mac and cheese at least three times a week and walked most places because he couldn't afford a needed vehicle repair. Jason had no right. None. But the twitch in the man's jaw indicated the jury had deliberated and given their judgment.

The words of the apostle Luke in 12:11-12 came to

mind. *When they bring you before the synagogues and the rulers and the authorities, do not be anxious about how you should defend yourself or what you should say, for the Holy Spirit will teach you in that very hour what you ought to say.*

Sure, Owen wasn't in front of the synagogue or the rulers, but Jason held authority in this church. This applied. The Holy Spirit was Owen's helper, and boy, did he need help. Right now. In this *very hour*.

Give me words and humility.

Owen held Jason's gaze and refused to flinch. "I understand the church has been here before and that means you have to ask the tough questions. I will not take this personally. I want you to do whatever you have to do to be confident that I've committed no wrong."

Jason's eyes widened. His posture, which had been tense and ready for a fight, relaxed a little. It wasn't much, but it was enough to give Owen the confidence that he was on the right track.

"You have my permission to ask whatever you want, look into my personal finances, and poke around my private life. I have nothing to hide."

"I appreciate that, Pastor. This isn't easy."

"I don't imagine it is."

And while they investigated Owen, it gave him time to do his own digging, because when they cleared him, there'd be a witch hunt. And the only way to protect the unity of the church was to uncover the thief himself.

"I'll be in touch about our next steps." Jason held out his hand.

Owen stood, accepted his hand, shook, and nodded. As the door closed behind Jason, he fell back into his chair and cradled his head. *Lord, help us.*

Before he could pray another word, his inbox dinged with a message from Clara, marked as urgent.

His heart sank further. Gloria had given Tommy a treat with red dye, something he wasn't allowed to have. Apparently, Tommy's parents had called Clara to complain. The boy had bounced off the walls all night long. There was no grace in Clara's tone, but to be fair, tone was hard to read in an email.

He started to type a reply about how this was the happiest he'd seen the choir, well, ever. But Clara's lengthy explanation about how the job of the choir was to sing, not make crafts and eat treats, slowed his fingers.

Maybe if the same kids didn't get the large roles every year . . . Backspace and delete.

Questioning her direction wouldn't help. Clara always put on a respectable show. But frankly, the only kids who ever looked like they had fun were the same crew that starred year after year.

Another email dinged.

Gloria.

He saved his response to Clara as a draft and opened Gloria's message.

Several parents called Gloria to say that the last practice was the most fun their children had at choir in years.

Years! Gloria was convinced that Clara would have to give her the recommendation.

He closed her email without answering, pressed a shaky hand to his forehead, and sagged. His gaze dropped to the text he'd been preparing for Sunday. In Acts 6:10-15, after Stephen spoke, the people couldn't withstand it.

So, they killed him.

Chapter Eleven

The next few weeks flew by in what Gloria could only describe as a blurred frenzy of activity. A single scene failed to stand out in her mind, just chaotic moment after chaotic moment, split between helping Meg with wedding plans and preparing the kids to be the best, most unique, most *involved* choir this town had ever seen. This wasn't a group of tiny humans regulated to the back, dressed to blend in with the scenery. Nope. They were front and center for their songs. Just as needed to the plot as the main actors.

Gloria had taken the words *complete freedom* to heart and steered this play as she saw fit. Only a small twinge of apprehension twanged, warning her she might have pushed too hard and too far. But later, when Clara and Gloria got the entire group together for a dress rehearsal, the woman would have to agree. It was the exact kind of unexpected twist the musical—and the kids—needed.

It was a good idea.

In theory.

Her gut twisted more.

Breanna had perfected the solo dance that Gloria choreographed, pulling from her younger years of ballet and jazz. Luke was the bee that his little brother absolutely refused to dress as because, as Bethann said, all bees are stupid. And the twins shifted between flowers and stars, depending on the song.

Adorable. Ab-so-lu-tely a-dor-a-ble.

She hadn't planned on focusing so much on the Clarke kids, but when Owen released the fall schedule, she suspected that Nathan had hoped for more opportunities to keep his kids busy. Her non-position in the community didn't give her an avenue to officially help out Nathan with his kids, so she shifted gears. She could give his kids bigger roles that would extend their practice hours so Nathan could have a bit more time to himself. She could use that one-on-one time with them to inject as much fun and laughter back into their life as possible. She could show his kids, and all the others that had believed the lie they were nothing but wallflowers, that they had something more to offer. Something valuable. Something no one else brought to the table. Something she desperately needed to hear as a young girl while her big sister collected first place medals, and Gloria collected participation ribbons. She'd even gone as far as to pull out her old rhyming book.

You are the you that you need to be. No one else can be

you, no one else, no siree. If we didn't have you, we'd be missing a lot. You matter. You're wanted. Your company's sought.

She repeated her mantra to the choir so many times they probably thought it was one of their songs.

In a way, it was.

It was her song also. She had something Sycamore Hill Community Church needed. They just didn't know it yet.

"Thanks again for picking me up." Gloria hopped into her sister's car and pulled the vehicle door closed quickly before any more rainwater could leak in.

"Anytime." Jessica revved the engine and pulled out of the courthouse parking lot.

If only it were as easy for Gloria to pull the door of her mind closed on all the things her mother said to her this morning before she left the house. Today was her final court appearance in the trial against Emergence. The attorney had been correct, and Gloria was recalled to the stand. But it was Mom's comments that rattled Gloria, distracting her during the closing arguments in the case. When her insides should've been singing with the brilliant conclusion to the drug scandal story, all she could hear was:

Has Owen made his intentions toward you clear?

You're not as young as you used to be. You don't have time to waste.

Translation: Tell that boy to pick up his feet and put a ring on your finger before your uterus expires.

Gloria clicked her seatbelt together and rubbed her thumb over her bare fourth finger on her left hand.

Have the kids learned their songs yet?

Is Clara writing that reference?

Translation: Why are you rocking the boat? Just do things the way Clara expects and be done with it. You can't turn this ship, so just get in and row.

Gloria shifted in her seat, trying to get comfortable in a skirt and blouse that suddenly felt too tight. Mom meant well. But the playfulness in her tone couldn't erase the unspoken implication. Sycamores were go-getters. They accomplished great things. They reached goals. What Sycamores didn't do was get kicked out of school and accused of a crime, change career tracks halfway through university, or struggle to find work.

Unless your first name was Gloria.

Never-good-enough-Gloria.

Gloria didn't have the heart or the willpower to continually challenge her mom. She'd spent the last nine months proving her innocence to the judge and jury, and she was done. Finished. She had nothing left. Her ketchup bottle spurted dust over the French fries of life. The container was empty.

"How did court go?" Jessica flicked her wipers to high speed, checked her blind spot, and changed lanes.

"The closing was fantastic. The attorney did a great job." Now all she had to do was wait for the jury to decide the company's fate. Then, she could put Emergence, Tiff, and the scandal behind her.

"I meant, how was it for you?" Her sister kept her attention on the ever-slickening road, but genuine concern for Gloria oozed from her tone.

The soft beating of the wipers moved back and forth over the windshield in sync with Gloria's heartbeat. It soothed her. "Honestly, it was lousy. The defense made me out to be some sort of disgruntled employee trying to score a quick buck."

Jessica's eyes got that look. The same look she wore when she stepped between Gloria and a bully in elementary school. The same look she wore when Tiff made a passing comment about being innocent in the scandal that wrecked Gloria's life. It shot fire and ice, ready to fight to the death for her kid sister. In proper Sycamore fashion, Jessica stood in the gap with her weapon loaded. "You knew going in that it was gonna be hard, right? The prosecuting attorney prepared you, right?"

"Yeah, she did." But that didn't make it any easier to swallow. No one liked to hear their name dragged through the mud, and the last thing Gloria needed was for a church member to latch onto the crazy notion that she was out for revenge or looking to cash in.

But, of course, they would read it. Everyone in town followed the trial. Everyone had an opinion. Everyone was keeping score.

And no matter what the judge decided about Emergence Pharmaceuticals or her old roommate, Tiff, Gloria was losing. Bad. Gloria felt the weight of Jessica's gaze.

"I get the feeling you think you deserve everything that happened to you."

Pain shot through her jaw, and Gloria unclenched her teeth.

"God has some good words for those who feel like they don't deserve His kindness."

Gloria counted the trees they passed.

"It's not your fault."

Fourteen, fifteen, sixteen.

"You're made in the image of God. For that reason alone, you deserve kindness."

Nice try. Pretty soon Jessica would fall back to the old *God don't make no junk* phrase made popular on cat posters and memes.

"Look at me." Jessica's tone demanded that Gloria stop counting trees. Jessica waited until Gloria turned her face toward her sister. "We love you. We are here for you."

Gloria forced her features into a smile. It was nice of Jessica, but that was a quick fix. Only temporary. Besides this wasn't about her family's acceptance. It wasn't even about God's acceptance. It was about learning to live with the shame that came from the scandal. The shame of never being good enough.

Jessica studied her for an uncomfortable minute, then switched gears. "What's wrong with your car?"

The tightness in Gloria's chest eased. "Nothing.

Owen's truck wouldn't start, so I lent him mine. He had a bunch of appointments that he couldn't miss."

"Hmm." Jessica kept her attention on the road as the lights of the city faded behind them. She'd mastered Mom's skill of saying nothing while simultaneously saying everything at the top of her lungs.

Mom didn't trust Gloria's judgment when it came to people, her future, or well, anything. That was the problem with moving back home. Your adulthood got packed away with your stuff, and suddenly, your parents had an opinion on every part of your life. But Jessica? Sisters weren't supposed to judge. They stood with you, shoulder to shoulder in solidarity against parental attacks. At least, that's what a sister was supposed to do.

It was exhausting being the black sheep of the family. *Exhausting*.

A tiny noise erupted from the back of her throat, and Jessica cut her gaze Gloria's way and changed the topic again.

"How are things with Owen?"

"Complicated."

Jessica lifted her eyebrows.

"It's like there's a cloud hanging over him ever since the funds for the roof went missing."

Her sister let out a low whistle. "Have they made any progress? Does Owen suspect anyone?"

Gloria shrugged. She loved that her sister didn't once think that Owen might be guilty. No one in her family even tolerated the idea for one second. It almost made up for their micromanaging ways and strong opinions. "He said that Suzy was in the office after the potluck."

"Jason's wife? I heard they're having trouble."

Gloria sat upright in the bucket seat. "Marriage trouble?"

Jessica shrugged. "We aren't close or anything, but I know money is tight."

Accusing the Chalkeys with no evidence was just as bad as Jason accusing Owen without grounds. Gloria changed the subject as they crossed Sycamore Hill's town line. "How's my favorite brother-in-law?"

"Hopeful." Jessica's face glowed with a secretive brilliance.

Gloria stilled. "Are you pregnant?" Tate and Jessica had been trying to get pregnant for over a year. Jessica had already lost two babies in miscarriages, and since then, struggled with infertility. Emma opening up her walk-in clinic was a gift from the hand of God. Now Jessica had someone local with medical know-how to talk with about her struggles.

Now it was Jessica's turn to shrug. "Maybe. Hopefully."

"Have you taken a test?"

Jessica flattened her lips. She blinked rapidly, so rapidly that when she didn't answer right away, Gloria let it slide.

After a few silent minutes, Jessica cleared her throat. "I ordered two tests online, but both were duds."

"Maybe you peed on the stick wrong."

Jessica snorted.

"Let's get another one. Right now."

"I can't."

The benefit of being the passenger instead of the driver meant that Gloria could watch her sister's every move. The muscles in Jessica's throat contracted as she swallowed. Her rapid blinking, the stiffness of her neck, the way she gripped the steering wheel so hard that her knuckles turned white told a story.

"What do you mean, *can't*?"

"People know we've been struggling to get pregnant. If they see me buy another test, then I'm going to have to answer questions. That's why I ordered online. If I get a local one and the test is negative—"

"I get it. You're not ready to answer questions."

"More like I shouldn't have to answer questions. But hey." She laughed. "That's small-town life."

Jessica's hollow chuckle hurt Gloria's heart. Here she was moaning about a smear to her name when her sister was dealing with literal life and death issues. "Wouldn't you rather know?"

"Of course, I would." Jessica snapped. She cut her eyes to Gloria. "Sorry." She folded her lips inward. "But if it's positive and I miscarry again, I can't go through that. Having to let everyone know. Having to correct people who congratulate us." A tear popped from the corner of her eye and slid down her cheek.

Gloria had no real understanding of how traumatic this past year had been on her sister. Living in the city had insulated her from much of Jessica's turmoil. She didn't want to be insulated anymore. She wanted to be there for her sister the way Jessica was trying to be there for her. The brightly-lit Sycamore Pharmacy sign flickered ahead. "Pull in."

Jessica pulled into the parking lot of the drug store and cut the engine. The rain pinged off the roof of the cab. "What are you doing?"

"Getting you some answers." Gloria hopped out of the vehicle, pulled her jacket up over her head, and jogged into the store. Jessica deserved to know.

The young cashier lifted her head as the door jingled the string of bells hanging from the frame. "Good evening."

Gloria nodded. She didn't know the cashier, which meant the cashier didn't know Gloria. Score one for anonymity.

Gloria trolled the aisles until she found the contraceptives and pregnancy tests. The irony of stocking them side by side on the shelf hit her as ridiculous. She glanced at the curved circular mirror that exposed shoplifters. The cashier's head jerked away.

Nosy Nora.

Gloria pulled a Quick Results test, but it wouldn't come off the shelf. Darn. It was locked. They did this in the city, locked the contraceptives and pregnancy tests to prevent theft, but she hadn't expected that in Sycamore Hill.

The bells above the door jingled, and Mrs. Brisbane's

voice carried back to Gloria. "Good evening, Chantelle." Her footsteps grew louder.

Gloria's dinner flip-flopped. She tracked Mrs. Brisbane in the anti-theft mirror. She'd be rounding the corner any second.

Gloria slipped around the corner into the next aisle. Feminine Hygiene. Well at least shopping in this aisle meant no one would think she was pregnant. She moved soundlessly toward the exit. Three more steps to freedom, and her gaze collided with her sister's hopeful one through the vehicle windshield. Gloria froze. Jessica deserved to know.

Gloria held up a finger to indicate that she'd be another minute. Mrs. Brisbane added a few items to her basket and meandered around the corner. Gloria's corner.

She zipped down the next aisle and tried to control her breathing in this weird game of cat and mouse. Gloria pressed her back against the shelving. Her chest heaved. She couldn't leave the store empty-handed. She spun around and slammed right into the cashier.

The young girl's forehead puckered, and her arms were folded across her middle. "Can I help you?"

Gloria tracked Mrs. Brisbane that tiny mirror. She was on the move again. "No, I'm just browsing." Gloria edged around another corner. The cashier followed.

"If you're not going to buy anything, I need you to leave."

"Everything okay over there, dear?" Mrs. Brisbane's voice increased in volume.

No, Lord, please, no.

"It's fine, thanks," the cashier called.

The older woman poked her head around the corner and Gloria quickly tipped hers forward so her hair covered her face. The last thing she needed was Mrs. Brisbane reporting to the hens that Gloria was a suspected shoplifter.

Gloria dropped her voice to a whisper. "I need an item that's locked, in the next aisle, but I want to wait until the other shopper is gone."

Understanding lit the girl's eyes. She nodded. She returned to her post at the checkout and rang through Mrs. Brisbane's items. Their murmured words didn't make it back to Gloria, but she caught their good-bye.

Gloria sagged against the merchandise shelving.

Chantelle met Gloria in the family planning aisle. "What do you need?" Her clipped tone had dropped a few degrees from her sympathetic gaze just moments before. The previous compassion in her eyes had vanished.

Gloria pointed to the pregnancy tests.

Chantelle silently unlocked the items and Gloria pulled the closest one from the shelf. No wonder her sister didn't want to do this. Gloria didn't even know this girl, and the judgment oozing from her made Gloria feel dirty.

But she'd done nothing wrong. Gloria lifted her chin.

She had nothing to be ashamed of. She had every right to make this purchase and she didn't owe anyone an explanation. Gloria sailed to the cash and placed the item on the counter.

Chantelle followed. She scanned the test. Her eyes paused on Gloria's ringless left hand. That's right, Gloria thought, giving her fingers a wiggle. No ring. And it's none of your business.

"Would you like a bag?"

Really? After hiding in the store, the girl thought Gloria would walk out holding the test proudly to save a measly ten cents? "Yes, please."

"I, ah, noticed you're not married."

"That's wildly inappropriate to point out."

Chantelle's eyes flashed. "I'm inappropriate? You're the one dating the pastor and buying a pregnancy test."

Lightheadedness overwhelmed Gloria. The cashier moved in and out of focus. Gloria stretched her eyes wide open to try and gain clarity. "I'm not," she croaked. "It's not for me."

The girl looked pointedly at the bag in Gloria's hand and pinched her features.

Gloria glanced out the window at the car in the parking lot. Her sister waited. Her sister who needed her privacy. Her perfect sister. The one who always pleased her parents, always did what was right, always performed flawlessly finally needed her.

Lord, help me.

Gloria swallowed her pride, lowered her head, and

walked out. She sucked in a deep breath of the cool evening air, but it failed to cool the furnace in her chest. The rain plastered her hair to her head, but she no longer hurried. Somehow, she doubted that Owen would find this as amusing as her dress mishap. She had to get in front of this.

As she passed the only other parked car in the lot, the headlights flicked on. The sidewalk lit like a stage on which Gloria was the star, illuminating her face before she could turn away. Only shadows moved behind the glare. She kept walking.

A quick glance back revealed Nettie Fry on a cell phone. Her lips flapped a mile a minute.

So much for getting out in front of this.

Chapter Twelve

The toe of Owen's boot caught the edge of something, and his arms shot out at the sides to balance him. His to-go coffee cup hit the gravel in the church parking lot. Dark liquid saturated the fabric of his pant leg. He fisted his hands. What had he tripped on? A slice of roofing material.

Several pieces of roofing, to be more precise. Asphalt shingles spotted the property, buried in the grass, pushed up against the brick exterior, and scattered here and there across the parking lot. The sun broke through the clouds, making it easier to evaluate the damage on the peaked roof of the church. The storm from the previous evening had peeled back fresh layers of shingles in several new places, revealing rotted plywood.

Owen unlocked the church doors and grabbed a fistful of industrial sized garbage bags from under the kitchen sink. His mind spun in several directions. Would tarping the sound equipment provide enough protection from the water that was certain to pour in after the next clap of thunder? How many computers were in danger of water damage? And the worst, the church wouldn't be able to meet in the building until the roof was fixed.

He sliced the plastic bags open at their seams with a knife from the kitchen and covered the sound equipment at the back of the sanctuary. He used a few hymnals to weigh down the edges, carefully folding the books under the protection of the plastic so no one could accuse him of ruining the books. He then covered Janet's desktop computer tower, monitor, and keyboard. Owen worked from a laptop that was safely stowed in his satchel, so all he did was poke his head into his office to ensure nothing was out in the open that could be damaged.

His phone! A breath whooshed out. He'd thought he'd misplaced it last night. He snagged it from the desktop and stuffed it into his back pocket without looking at it.

After locking the office door, something he never did before the theft, he hurried outside to start cleaning up. As he stuffed shingle after shingle into the bag, he prayed. *Lord, I don't know what you are trying to teach me, but I have to believe You have a plan. You are not pacing back and forth in heaven, wringing your hands, wondering what to do about the accusations against me, the damage to the church, or about the congregation reeling from a second betrayal. I want to say use me however you see fit, but my flesh wants to be vindicated. I want the people to know I'm innocent. I don't want to leave with this accusation hanging over my head, casting a shadow on the rest of my life.*

Like it did for Gloria.

Irony hit. Now that Gloria was back in town and the trial was leaning favorably toward backing her story and officially clearing her name, Owen might be pushed out.

Thunder rumbled, and a chill zipped down his back. Leaves blew free from the nearby trees. The naked branches rustled. He stuffed another shingle into the bag. The seam split.

It wasn't supposed to be this hard.

Owen stopped. He stopped everything. His frantic actions. His runaway thoughts. His attempts to fix the church, Gloria, and perceptions of the congregation. When had he embraced the idea that ministry was supposed to be easy? Jesus didn't promise heaven on earth now. Heaven came later. Right now, Jesus said there would be trouble and suffering. Somewhere along the way, Owen had rejected the idea that random hardship and misery hit everyone. And now, he reaped the disastrous harvest of such a denial. The people in the church simply didn't know what to do when confronted with sin and suffering any more than he did.

Lord, I'm struggling to not just respond well, but also suffer well. I'm tired of jumping through hoops to please people. I'm weary and want to give up. I'm drained by emotional conversations driven by fear. Suffering has brought out our worst. It's exposed weakness and sin.

He dropped to his knees in the middle of the lawn in front of the church. The grass, still damp from the rain, soaked through his pants. He didn't care who saw him. He didn't care who might drive by. This was about him and the Lord. It was about figuring out what it meant to set aside his rights and freedoms to love his brothers and sisters well, even if he suffered as a result. How he represented Christ in the midst of his suffering mattered. *Lord, I want to remove all obstacles to the gospel of Christ, even if that obstacle is me.*

The theft of the funds arrived like smelling salts, making the congregation aware of lingering bitterness and trust issues. It was Owen's job to lead the congregation into repentance for as long as the good Lord gave him opportunity.

His fingers loosened on the ripped bag. With his head tipped back and eyes closed he whispered, "Not my will, but yours be done."

Janet's tiny, compact vehicle pulled into the parking lot. She grabbed a shoulder bag from the backseat and picked her way toward him, avoiding the wreckage.

He stood, brushing away the debris stuck to his wet pants.

She crinkled her nose as she surveyed the lawn. "This doesn't look good."

"Depending on what those clouds do"—Owen gestured to the gray gathering in the sky—"it might get worse before it gets better. I'm not sure where the water is going to pour in. I've covered the electronics with plastic already."

"Would you like me to call anyone?"

Owen didn't really want another confrontation with the deacon board, but this wasn't something he could keep from them. They'd need to make a decision about how to proceed, especially since they no longer had the funds. "Jason, please."

A flush crept across Janet's cheeks. Her head dipped, and she developed an intense interest in the nearest shingle, poking it with the toe of her shoe. "He's already on his way."

Owen's stomach heaved. Something about the way Janet shuffled her feet and avoided his gaze didn't sit well. The air around them stilled. The leaves settled on the grass in an eerie lull. Even the birds quieted. Something was coming down the pipeline, and Owen was standing at the mouth of the tube.

"What's going on?"

Janet rubbed the back of her neck. Her chest rose and fell, and she swallowed excessively. She didn't hold his gaze for more than a second before flicking it away. However, it was long enough for him to read disappointment in her eyes.

"Jason called me when I was on my way in. Someone from church saw Gloria buying a pregnancy test, and they also saw her car overnight at your house."

He instinctively stepped back, craving physical and emotional distance, but not having the luxury.

A low rumble rolled across the sky. The wind scooped up the leaves, and a wet mist chapped Owen's cheek. He turned to face the sudden breeze. It cupped over his ears and echoed. He misheard Janet. That had to be it. His tongue bumped along his lips but failed to relieve the dryness overtaking his mouth. Dullness filled his chest as he fixated on the spire on the summit of the church. An optical illusion made it appear to sway.

"My truck broke down, and I can't afford the repair, so Gloria lent me her car." He pointed to Gloria's vehicle in the church parking lot. "I've been driving it for a few days now."

Understanding filled Janet's eyes as her eyebrows gathered in. "That makes more sense. Hank Sinclair called to ask if Gloria was distracting you at work because he saw her vehicle in the lot every time he drove by. And since I'm not here every day..." Her words trailed off.

"People thought I was alone with Gloria," Owen finished. So much for getting the benefit of the doubt.

Janet nodded. She wouldn't meet his eye. "What about the other thing?" Her chest stilled like she held her breath. Did she really think so little of him? Did she really think he'd stand at the pulpit every Sunday and preach a message that he failed to apply to his own heart?

She tilted her head, waiting.

Apparently, she did.

The wet mist fattened into a drizzle. Owen tugged the hood from his thick sweatshirt over his head. "Gloria had some meetings in the city about the court case. Her sister drove her—"

Her sister drove her.

Jessica and Tate had been trying to get pregnant for well over a year. Gloria must have bought the test for Jessica, to save her sister the humiliation of answering a million questions from a busybody community.

Janet leaned in. Waiting.

Owen wasn't about to out Gloria's sister. Not on a hunch. And not even if he knew one hundred percent that his suspicions were true. If Gloria bought the pregnancy test to protect Jessica, then Owen would honor that choice. "I don't know about that. I can only assure you that I have treated Gloria with the utmost respect, and she is an honorable woman."

Dampness seeped into Janet's eyes, creating a faint sheen. "I knew it couldn't be true. I'm sorry."

"It's not your fault." It was his, and it was time he owned it. The reality was that pastors are held to a higher standard because God has entrusted to them a responsibility for which they are accountable. But he'd been too busy trying to please the people, earn their approval, and prove he was worthy of the title pastor. He'd forgotten who all this was for. Shame descended. Fear instead of freedom.

There is no condemnation for those who are in Christ Jesus.

Conviction? Yes. Condemnation? No.

I'm sorry for how my actions and reactions might have tarnished Your name.

A strange buoyancy lifted him. God was more than able to defend His name, clear up the misunderstanding about Gloria, and expose the thief who smeared Owen's reputation. God could restore this church with a single Word. Owen didn't need to micromanage God. It was long past time that he released it all into the Lord's capable hands to do with as He saw fit. How God saw fit. Not Owen.

Janet's attention bounced all over the property. Her nose wrinkled like she smelled something terrible. "I'm sorry, because it gets worse."

The drizzle expanded into drops. Big, fat drops that splatted at their feet.

"Jason is coming to tell you that the board has decided to remove Gloria from the play. They've decided the constant scandal that surrounds her makes her an inappropriate role model."

Jason's truck turned into the lot and parked, perfectly timed. The bill of his ball cap shadowed his grim expression, but the hard set of his jaw and jerky head movements indicated slapping the scarlet A on Gloria's chest and calling her Hester was merely a formality.

The sky broke open. Rain pellets hit the ground. Janet yelped and dashed for the church doors. Owen followed. He waited in the foyer, rainwater dripping down his face, holding the door for his executioner.

Chapter Thirteen

G loria moved the musical rehearsal to her parents'
barn at Clara's prompting. The church was a
sopping mess. She could have cancelled practice, but it
was the last one before the performance, and Gloria
wanted to do everything she could to ensure her little
stars shone. Besides, she needed to keep busy, or she'd
give in to the temptation to call Owen and see how he
was managing. But he didn't need to be fielding calls
from her. Not with the roof money gone and rising flood
waters rippling across the sanctuary.

Owen would reach out when he could. Until then,
she'd push on with her kids and ensure the storm didn't
derail their performance. Besides, she'd have to tell Owen
about her blunder at the pharmacy if she connected with
him. The pressure in her head increased just recalling the
cashier's brazen words, her accusing stare, and Nettie Fry
on the phone, reporting the news.

Gloria gulped. How could she have been so stupid to go into the *local store* and buy a pregnancy test? She could justify it six ways to Sunday, and it wouldn't change a thing. Her impulsivity bred foolishness, which spawned consequences—unavoidable ones. Appearances mattered. Her reputation mattered because it affected Owen. So she had to confess what she'd done and seek Owen's forgiveness for how it was bound to impact his job. And that conversation needed more than five distracted minutes while he trekked church valuables to higher ground.

It wasn't avoidance. It was wisdom—the opposite of foolishness.

"Beautiful, Breanna." Gloria distracted herself, lightly touching Breanna's shoulder. Breanna extended her leg and bent at the hips, her arms long and graceful. She wore a new leotard that made her look like a real ballerina. It was good. She needed something positive to pour herself into.

Gloria continued to wander, checking in on the various clusters of children working out their parts. Ribbons rippled, carrying laughter along their currents. Everything was just as it should be.

Meg and Emma took the smallest of the crew into the house for a snack. Gloria's mom thrived in her element, surrounded by the choir of garden flowers and evening stars, feeding their bodies and probably their souls the same way she once fed Gloria and Owen after school. But this snack—Gloria had ensured—contained no red dye. No dairy. No nuts. No gluten. No sugar. And, if pressed, Gloria would add, no taste.

"Gloria?"

She lifted her head. Clara stood at the entrance to the barn by the enormous open door. Her age-spotted hands twisted in front of her thick middle, and her face puckered sourly.

Jason stepped around her.

Ah, the lemon in the flesh.

He immediately surveyed the space as if Gloria might inflict some sort of damage on the children under her care.

Gloria huffed. For heaven's sake. Suzy must have spun some tale to cause Jason to track her down like a papa bear on steroids.

"What can I do for you?" As Gloria crossed toward them, the choir spilled in behind Clara and Jason. They split around them and came together again on the other side like a swarm of bees. They buzzed for her attention.

"I'll listen to each one of you if you can talk one at a time, but first, I need to speak with Mr. Chalkey and Mrs. Brisbane."

Her mom, Meg, and Emma herded the kids to the side. "Let's practice the garden song," Mom said.

Emma added, "I've heard you've all made beautiful flower masks."

The children hurried to do their bidding.

"I'm sorry, Gloria." Mrs. Brisbane's rapid blinking couldn't hide her wet eyes.

Sorry? She turned to Jason and arched a brow.

He cleared his throat, and his Adam's apple bobbed. "I'm here to notify you that you've been removed from the play. Effective immediately."

"What?" Everything slowed down, like smoke slogging through her veins. She must have misheard.

Her mom's head lifted, a curious expression pointed at Jason.

"I don't understand." Gloria ignored her mother's unspoken question and sought Clara, who glared at Jason.

Jason's features contorted into annoyance. He jerked his chin up as if to nudge Clara.

"Not a chance." Clara folded her arms across her body. "This is your show. I've already said my piece."

Gloria's insides hummed as if the buzzing students swarmed under her skin. A soft waft of her mom's signature scent bolstered Gloria's courage. Meg joined them. The solidarity emboldened her. Gloria held Jason's stare. She was not speaking first. Not making whatever this was easier.

Jason cleared his throat a second time. His gaze flicked behind her, then to Meg, and landed on her again. "It's come to our attention that you and Owen have been inappropriate." His features tightened." And intimately involved."

Her mom's sharp intake momentarily caught Jason's attention before it bounced back to Gloria. "We cannot have a person of ill repute running our children's programs."

The room fuzzed. Gloria's skull filled with cotton swabs. Her ears throbbed, and she grabbed for the barn-board walls. Romantically involved? They think— Her cheeks burned. Of course, they did. Not once had anyone given her the benefit of the doubt. That she could handle. That she had made her peace with. But to say this about Owen? To smear his name over a piece of gossip before checking the facts?

Twenty pairs of little eyes stuck to her like glue. Twenty impressionable children. Little souls shaped by the adults around them. They waited on her. Waited to see if, when tested, she'd emerge as gold or burn like dross.

She could feel her mother straighten behind her, charging the air like a lightning strike. "Who do you think you are?"

"Mom, don't." Gloria didn't need her mother esca-lating things in front of the kids, who Emma was thankfully ushering out the side door. Was this God's way of nudging her along? Of confirming she wasn't the one for Owen? Or was this the enemy testing her? Was Owen's church on the verge of a spiritual revival, and all this a distraction? If the cost of reviving this community was her reputation, did she love the people of Sycamore Hill—love the Lord enough—to joyfully pay it? And if not, what did that say about her?

She inhaled until her lungs filled. Nothing held her in

Sycamore Hill. She was not obligated to this town. Self-righteous thoughts piled. Unspoken words burned the inside of her mouth. Graceless words about Pharisees, legalism, and gossip. Hands that shed innocent blood, hearts that devised wicked plans, feet that ran to evil: the Lord hated those things. The Lord hated those who sowed discord in his church.

But that passage in Proverbs also said the Lord hated haughty eyes. Arrogance. A person who looked down on another. The Lord hated it all.

Including her pride.

Her eyes prickled. Gloria swallowed bitterness. "You're wrong, Jason. Wrong to dismiss me without first having a conversation. Wrong to have said that in front of the children. Wrong to assume the worst about Owen."

His jaw twitched. The only indication the man before her wasn't made of stone. The muscle throbbed with a steady pulse.

She wasn't innocent. She got that now. Hadn't she looked down on Suzy and Nettie? Hadn't she hardened herself against them? Hadn't she made thoughtless decisions? She could call it self-defense. She could excuse it and justify it. But if Christ died for her while she was still sinning, couldn't she continue to love others even while they continued to sin against her? Isn't that what Christ-like love was all about?

"I have nothing to be ashamed of, but I do owe you" —she swept her gaze to include her mom, Clara, and Meg—"an explanation."

Her mom shook her head, but Gloria didn't need another excuse to put herself first. After coming home, she'd nudged God from the center of her life and inserted herself in the middle. Everything revolved around her. She needed a job. She needed a reference. She needed to help Jessica. She needed the courts to vindicate her. She needed to prove her worth. The common denominator in all her strivings was her. But nothing she could ever do would make her worthy. If it could, Christ wouldn't have had to die. Her worthiness came not from making a name for herself but from her union with Christ.

Why had it taken her so long to see that?

Her eyes misted at how God used the actions of the Suzys and Netties of the world to peel her eyes off herself and force them back onto Him. God won't share His glory with another.

"I never asked what would be helpful. I just acted. I never paused to seek God's will. That seed of pride grew sin in my heart." She levelled her gaze at Jason. "And for that, I am sorry. Of that, I repent. But the tawdry suggestions you're making here are completely unfounded."

Jason never broke eye contact. He held her stare, fully convinced that he was acting in the church's best interests. He'd already made the decision. She was out.

Gloria rolled her lips in and pressed them together. She wasn't going to cry. Not in front of the children. *Your will be done, Lord.* She handed the folder in her hand to Clara. "All my notes are in there. You'll have everything you need to finish the play."

Clara accepted the folder. Her lower lip trembled, but she remained silent. She didn't need to say anything. Her face and stiff posture radiated displeasure. Whether she directed that displeasure toward Gloria, Owen, or Jason, she couldn't tell. But honestly, it didn't matter.

Gloria was done.

Chapter Fourteen

The phone call was quick, succinct, and devastating. Owen disconnected and slumped in a chair at his kitchen table. He cradled his head in his hands. Jason hadn't given him a chance to prep Gloria. Hadn't allowed him to be there for the woman he loved while the people who were supposed to care for her spiritual well-being—the local church leaders—humiliated her.

Meg called minutes after Gloria left the barn. He'd hung up after speaking with her, and Emma rang. If nothing else, Gloria's faithful friends rallied around her.

A gift from God amid ruin. A bright spot in the shadows.

God, what are you doing?

His repeated phone calls to Gloria went directly to voice mail. He understood screening calls. He understood needing time, but shutting him out? He wanted—

he needed—to be part of the solution. To be there for her. But he worked for the very people that thrust the dagger of scandal into her gentle heart.

It felt like a million years ago that he stood on the church lawn, broken before God. Yet, it was only this morning that he asked God to remove all the obstacles between the town folks and Christ. But it was one thing to fall on his sword. It was another thing entirely to sacrifice Gloria. That wasn't part of the deal.

Yet, her reputation lay slain, possibly beyond repair. His wasn't any better, but he cared less about that.

That's how Meg, Eli, Emma, and Ben found him. Face to the table. Bible open. Cheeks wet with tears. They crowded around his tiny kitchen that filled a quarter of his apartment. But unlike their typical games night, when hooting and hollering roused his landlord from below to remind him to be quiet, the room remained silent tonight. Their ministry to him was their presence, and it was enough to lift the stigma and shame temporarily. The only one missing was Gloria.

"Do you think they'll fire you?" Ben was the first to break the silence and to ask what everybody had to be thinking.

Owen shrugged. "Probably. They think I stole the roof money. This'll seal my coffin." But he didn't care about that. He cared about Gloria. Who, if his watch was correct, should be here any second. She'd finally answered his call and agreed to come over.

Knuckles rapped on the door and nudged it open at

the same time. "Are you sure I can come in?" Gloria's feet remained glued in the hallway. "I wouldn't want people to think we're fraternizing inappropriately." She pulled up short as she scanned the room. Her hands turtled into the sleeves of her favourite sweater. She hugged herself, hiding behind comfy clothes and a scowl. "Chaperones." Her head bobbed. "Probably a good idea."

Owen pushed the chair back and stood. He didn't get it. He had expected her to arrive in tears. Maybe shout in anger. But this quiet acceptance? He didn't know what to do with it.

Gloria snagged a soda from the fridge and claimed the last chair at the table. "Clara called."

To apologize, Owen hoped.

"She said the rest of the rehearsal went fine. Parents have already flooded her inbox with emails." She gulped back a long draw from the can.

The others might buy the act that Gloria was fine, but Owen saw through it. Her overly bright eyes, heaving chest, and lifted chin contradicted the acceptance she declared. Like a soldier pushing through, wounded, her brave mask never cracked.

"You okay?" Meg nudged Gloria's shoulder with hers.

Maybe they weren't buying what she was selling after all.

Gloria quickly swiped a hand across her eyes. "If I can survive Emergence, I'll survive this."

Meg frowned, and Gloria squirmed.

"That doesn't answer her question," Emma said.

Yeah, they definitely weren't picking up what she put down any more than he did.

"I'm not okay," she finally admitted, focused on her hands twisting around the soda. She kept her head down and rubbed her thumbs up and down the can. "But I will be."

"How do you bounce back from something like this?" The question popped out before Owen could censor it.

Gloria lifted her face. She searched his expression for something Owen couldn't provide. Not because he didn't want to, but because he didn't know what she needed. His gut told him his days were numbered. Overcoming might be possible, but he wasn't sure he wanted to. He wasn't sure he could continue to walk alongside the people who hurt the woman he loved more than anyone else in the world when he wasn't sure he could protect her from it happening again. He wasn't sure if he had what it took to stay. Seminary didn't prepare him for this.

Meg, Eli, Emma, and Ben all faded into the background. Right now, it was Owen and Gloria. And he instinctively understood that whatever she said next would impact him. Something inside her was different. The edge was gone.

"I won't bounce back, but I'll *come* back, because it's not about me." She bit the corner of her lip. "It's not about us, Owen. It never was. Not really. And as long as we keep making it about us, we'll be disappointed."

"What is it about?"

She shrugged. "Power. Control. God's sanctifying work in His people."

"So that's it?" Ben cut in. "They treat you like this, and there are no consequences?"

"Oh, there will be consequences." Owen had already fielded calls from Gloria's sister, ready to storm down to the church and tell off Jason. He'd heard from several parents concerned over Jason's public dismissal of Gloria, who'd won many hearts with her genuine love for the quieter and overlooked children. Even Nathan called, insisting something be done. There would be consequences. For sure. "If I've learned anything in ministry work," Owen said, "it's that God is more interested in shaping us to be like Jesus than He is in taking away the suffering."

Gloria pinched her eyes shut and inhaled through her nose. "Let's talk about something else. Have you made any progress on the lost money?"

"That depends." Owen cut his eyes to Ben. "Is this all off the record?"

Ben chuckled. "Nothing I hear tonight will end up in the paper."

"I've been making a list of all the people who are under financial strain." Owen retrieved a notepad from a drawer in the kitchen. "At the top are Jason and Suzy."

"He could be trying to divert attention from them to

cover their tracks." Emma ripped open a bag of chips Owen had thrown onto the table.

Meg shifted to grab a handful. She popped a chip in her mouth and crunched. "Nathan's financial issues are no secret."

"I can't imagine him doing something like this," Eli spoke quietly. "And I'm not super comfortable accusing people without cause."

"We are not accusing anyone," Owen said. "Just brainstorming. It doesn't leave this room."

"I have to be on list," Gloria said. "It's only fair to include everyone in financial straits. I'm out of a job and living with my parents."

"Hank Sinclair is on a fixed income," Ben added. "I heard that some kids stomped through his garden, and he didn't have the money to hire a landscaper."

"If we're throwing everyone under the bus, I'm trying to get more funding for the medical clinic," Emma said. It wasn't a secret that Emma's new clinic was far from financially secure. She 'd established it as soon as she was a fully qualified nurse practitioner, but it wasn't cheap.

Gloria's cheeks puffed out in an irritated breath. "If we are going to list every person with a financial need, the entire town will be suspect. There has to be a way to narrow the search."

"Maybe there is," Owen murmured. Out of all the people in Sycamore Hill with financial needs, only one family showed a significant improvement in their circum-stances.

Gloria's upturned face waited for him to explain. Her wide eyes searched him, and his stomach lurched. *How much, Lord? How much can one woman absorb?*

This was going to crush her.

Chapter Fifteen

Gloria couldn't stop joyful tears from sliding down her cheeks despite being tossed out of her own production and forced to hide in the corner like a punished child. Her rag-tag choir had morphed from breathing background props to equal stars on the stage. The kids were wonderful.

Well, almost all of them were wonderful.

Tommy pulled his shirt off in the middle of act two and swung it over his head like he was a cowboy trying to rope a calf, but Mrs. Brisbane took it in stride. And for the most part, so did the parents.

Breanna danced her solo flawlessly, and Gloria was sure she saw dampness in her father's eyes. But she couldn't be sure. Gloria's position in the shadowy back corner of her parent's barn didn't provide a great sight-line to Nathan Clarke.

Luke buzzed at all the right times in the low-budget

costume they made from a yellow pillowcase with painted black stripes. And the twins? Well, they were the stars. Literal stars in the night sky, standing on the bottom riser in the choir and holding high above their heads a hockey stick with a sparkly star taped to the blade. They waved it in time to the music, accomplishing a tiny miracle when they resisted the temptation to clap the sticks in a mock face-off as they had in rehearsals. And Bethann only mooned the audience once when she bent down to pick up her dropped star.

Families from the church filled her parents' barn and spilled out the doors and onto the grass. The cool night hadn't impacted attendance. Family after family sat on the makeshift seats crafted from bales of straw. It was Gloria's idea to cover the straw with flannel blankets and set them up in rows. Her addition of pumpkins, corn stalks, and other farm-friendly fall decor added to the barn's quaint ambiance. It had only taken Gloria about an hour to convince her parents to open their outdoor building to the church, which was also the new Sunday morning location until the deacons figured out how to address the worsening roof situation.

When Gloria's dad heard what had gone down between Gloria and the deacons, he'd come out swinging. And he wasn't the only one. Meg stepped in, insisting on giving a character reference. Emma had been working closely with Jessica, monitoring her brand-new pregnancy, and when she learned what *really* happened and that Gloria wasn't defending herself, she added her voice to the conversation. But it wasn't enough.

It was never enough.

"Are you good?" Meg asked.

Gloria quickly swiped a hand across her damp eyes. The action bought her a few extra minutes to think. Shame had been lying to her for so long, telling her that she was unworthy and alone, pulling her back to her old way of thinking that condemned her by association to Tiff. It said she would never be good enough. But the truth had something different to say, and Gloria was still grappling with it.

"I'm done living in self-protection." That was just a fancy word for unbelief. Her gaze skipped down the line of children returning to the stage for a second bow. "God has done too much in me for me to keep camping there."

The space thundered with applause and then teetered with laughter as Bethann accidentally mooned the audience a second time.

Jason took to the stage as the clapping died off to say a few kind words about the kids.

"That should be you up there." Meg folded her arms across her chest.

"It's fine," Gloria whispered. "I'm fine." She was better than fine. God had worked mightily in her heart since the deacons expelled her from the musical. God humbled Gloria, and He convicted her that it was time she stopped declaring God had made her this way and the church needed to accept her. The truth was, Gloria needed to compare who she was with who God had called her to be and change as necessary. Gloria wasn't innocent. Her impulsiveness and thoughtless actions had contributed to her struggles.

"Before we wrap up the evening," Jason said, "Tate Wilder has an announcement."

Gloria's head snapped at the mention of her brother-in-law. She raked her eyes over the crowd until she found her sister. Gloria shook her head. Jessica didn't have to do this.

Emma joined Meg and Gloria in the shadows. "It'll be okay." Emma pressed a hand against Gloria's upper arm.

Gloria hadn't been totally prepared for how hard it would be to return to Sycamore Hill. If given the chance, she would definitely have handled things differently, but what she wouldn't do, what she could never do, was tell anyone who she bought that pregnancy test for. Gloria wasn't present when Jessica miscarried and really needed her, but she was here now, and she'd do anything for her big sister.

"I think our church family is in need of good news, wouldn't you say?" Tate's jovial voice didn't need amplifying.

"No, no, no, no, no," Gloria rocked back and forth with one hand over her mouth, muffling her words.

Gloria hadn't told anyone but Owen. A fist squeezed her lungs. Owen kept her secret. He'd insisted he and Gloria were innocent but refused to provide details because it wasn't his story to tell. His resoluteness in the face of tremendous pressure made her love him even more. He valued Jessica's privacy more than his job and more than his reputation.

Gloria held Jessica's gaze. Jessica bobbed her head as if to say it was okay.

Meg and Emma reached for Gloria's hands.

"After years of trying to have a baby, Jessica and I are expecting!"

A cheer rolled like a wave gaining momentum, but Gloria's stomach heaved.

Tate carried on to clarify that Gloria had bought the pregnancy test for Jessica and that Gloria's vehicle was at Owen's overnight because she lent it to him while his was being repaired.

Tate's public announcement was a beautiful gesture. More than kind. But Gloria wasn't here to vindicate herself. She was here for one thing only. To support the people she loved. After everything that had been said about her, logic dictated that she should pack up her bags and leave. But she'd been down that road, and it led nowhere. This time, she'd see it through. This was about modelling perseverance and trust in the Lord. It was about putting her sister above herself. It was about standing beside Owen and speaking truth as God provided opportunity. Gloria wasn't about to slink away with her tail between her legs after spending the last few weeks lecturing the children on boldness and being proud of how God made them.

"Gloria." Emma poked her.

She snapped back to the present. Someone said her name. But it wasn't Emma, and it wasn't Tate.

It was Jason.

"Gloria, where are you?" Jason shielded his eyes against the makeshift stage lights. "The leadership of our church dealt with Gloria publicly when we removed her from the play, so we need to make it right publicly as well."

Gloria's joints weakened. Meg and Emma's hands moved from her hands to each elbow to provide support. They nudged her from the shadows and into the light.

Jason's gaze locked on hers. "You have my sincerest apology. Some people have been talking"—his eyes cut to his wife, who dropped her head—"and I want you to know that such talking stops today. We hope you can forgive us for assuming the worst and making a hard season of life even harder."

Gloria swallowed, but the lump in her throat wouldn't budge. She nodded her head.

"Pastor Owen, would you close us in prayer?"

She needed out. Fresh air. Freedom lay a few steps away. A tree bent in the breeze, beckoning her, and then a body blocked her escape.

A familiar body. A warm body.

"Where are you going?" He spoke as if his words were only for her. As if the entire congregation wasn't waiting for him to close the night in prayer. As if he had all the time in the world.

Owen.

Everything that had tilted sideways righted itself.

Owen entwined their fingers. He pulled her along to the front of the room. Gloria kept her eyes down. "I was afraid if anyone saw us together, you'd lose your job," she whispered.

The closer they got to the front of the barn, the quieter it grew. Conversations literally stopped. A murmur rippled through the throng.

"Gloria did this tonight." Owen gestured at the decorated barn while he studied her. Not in the familiar way that she understood, but in a quizzical way that said he didn't quite know what to make of her. "After we rejected her, judged her, and excommunicated her, she did this because she loves our kids, her God, and this town more than she loves herself. She suffered silently because she loves us."

Jaws loosened across the room, but none were slacker than Gloria's. Did Owen actually say that? Out loud? In front of everyone?

"God's plan for this church has included suffering, sometimes intense suffering. But that was always His plan A. He hasn't defaulted to a plan B, C, or D. I think I forgot that for a while. God takes no joy in our struggles, but He has ordained our lives from eternity past, and even when it doesn't feel good—when it doesn't feel fair—it's not an accident."

Gloria's heart throbbed in her ears.

"God's greatest concern for the people of Sycamore

Hill Community Church is not giving us a roof, repairing our reputations, or providing comfort. It's about teaching us to hate sin and turn to Him. And He'll use everything we face to accomplish that."

Owen faced Gloria fully. He scooped up both her hands in his. "Gloria Sycamore has suffered well. Not perfectly, but well." Owen's gaze sought Jason's. "Jason's humble and public plea for forgiveness is an example to us. We can learn from these two, if we're willing."

Mrs. Brisbane started a slow clap. Soon, others joined in.

Owen led the crowd in a closing prayer. Afterward, people broke apart to mingle.

Clara threaded her way toward Gloria, pulling her into a grandmotherly hug. "You did a tremendous job with the musical. It was perfect. I'm certain you'll get the job at the school and stay in Sycamore Hill where you belong."

"You're giving me the recommendation?" Gloria's eyes stretched. "But Tommy took his shirt off within ten minutes of starting the play."

Clara patted the air with her hands. "I sent the recommendation in days ago."

Days ago? Before Tate cleared her name in the pregnancy kerfuffle?

Mrs. Brisbane nattered on. "As for Tommy? Well, that's nine minutes longer than usual. It might be Tommy's record." The people closest to them tinkled with laugher.

Clara hugged Gloria again, not giving her time to sort through her conflicting emotions. "Maybe you can join Meg and me for our weekly Bible study? She mentioned you ladies were meeting regularly."

"I'd like that." The Lord was so gracious.

As soon as the attention moved on, Breanna found Gloria. "I'm glad you came," the girl said. "You should have been up there with Mrs. Brisbane."

"I didn't want to cause any more trouble for Owen. You—" Gloria placed her hands on Breanna's shoulders as she looked the girl up and down. "You were brilliant. Beautiful. Stunning. I don't have enough adjectives to capture it."

Breanna glowed. Gloria wasn't sure, but she thought she even saw a smear of light lip gloss on the girl's lips.

Gloria hesitated. She bit the inside of her cheek. She hated to do this, to spoil an evening that had been a magnificent victory for Breanna, but it couldn't be helped.

After Owen ruled out suspects for the theft one by one, he shared his suspicion about the one family in better financial shape. Gloria recalled all the people who might have heard her and Owen discussing the money, who might have heard where the money was stored. Who suddenly showed up in lip gloss, a new leotard, and a fresh haircut. "Breanna, I have to ask you something."

Breanna folded her arms across her body. A worried glance to her dad erased all doubt in Gloria's beaten-down heart. They'd found their thief.

"I think I understand why you took the money, but this is not the way the Lord wants to meet your needs."

"You said He provides in strange ways. And then I heard about this money just sitting there, and we needed it so much." Breanna clutched Gloria's hands. "Dad's trying, but he doesn't see it. Luca didn't even have underwear that fit him. We needed it."

Gloria met and held the girl's eyes. "I believe you need it, but this is not the way."

"What do you know about need?" Breanna gestured to the twinkle lights and portable heaters to ward off the autumn evening chill. "Your barn is nicer than our house."

"I know that all of us need to depend on God and wait on God, and that includes you. Owen could have lost his job."

Breanna's cheeks lost their pink hue.

"You didn't make this decision in a vacuum. It impacted the people around you."

"Are you going to tell?"

Gloria hesitated. "Not tonight."

Tonight, Breanna could have her moment to shine.

Chapter Sixteen

Gloria fisted her hands on her hips. She surveyed the jam-packed storage unit. Correction. Overflowing storage unit. But she didn't see the boxes she needed to sort. Her mind drifted from the task at hand.

A lot had happened since the musical. Gloria's throat closed up just thinking about it. Breanna confessed, and Nathan returned the funds. Nathan hadn't attended a church service since his wife died, but the congregation's gentle response to Breanna and their enthusiastic desire to help Nathan manage better had wooed his battered heart. His wife had to be rejoicing in Heaven over her husband's reengagement with the community and, Lord willing, his faith.

Thankfulness clogged the back of her throat, and she shifted her focus. It fell on the top half of the storage unit that still housed boxes she needed to sort. Gloria didn't have the upper body strength to get them down, and Owen was late.

Again.

Gloria tapped the auction app on her phone and scrolled to her listing. The items she'd already posted had bids that were climbing. An unexpected release of tension loosened her muscles. She'd convinced the church's fund-raising committee to let her take over their planned rummage sale and move it online. After Suzy explained their biggest hesitation had been that an online auction stopped people from coming into the church building and that their favorite part of the rummage sale was chatting with buyers, they compromised and set aside an entire Saturday for buyers to schedule their pick-ups in person. Everybody won. And if the sales trend continued, by the time Gloria added the rest of her contributions of big-name clothing, accessories, footwear, and purses to the auction, there would be enough money to pay a roofer to fix the church. She just needed to get the clothes in the box at the top of the stack.

Gloria pushed up the sleeves of her sweater and pressed her shoulder against a stack of boxes. They slowly scraped along the floor.

"Need a hand?" She heard Owen's smile, and it made her insides swell. The soles of his shoes scraped along the floor with a scuffing sound.

"Sorry I'm late." His apology caressed the back of her neck, and she shivered from the warmth of his breath. He wrapped his arms around her middle and tugged her until her back pressed against his chest.

"You're worth the wait." She turned in his arms and lifted her face. "Did Jason tell you about the benevolent fund?"

All the lines on his forehead softened as he looked down at her. Wonderment replaced his playful banter. "He told me *someone* received a generous settlement from the courts and donated it to the church."

Joy rippled down her spine. "There's enough to help out Nathan's family, and Jason and Suzy, and still have a cushion leftover to keep in reserve for future needs in the church family."

His neck bent forward. A tingle started in her chest. "And you want to donate it?"

Her lungs expanded to their fullest. "All of it."

He pressed his lips to her temple and a whisper warmed her earlobe. "You are amazing."

She tucked herself into his arms, resting her cheek against his chest. The steady thumping of his heart promised her that she'd come home for all the right reasons. He cinched his arms tighter and rested his chin on the top of her head. They fit perfectly like that for several glorious seconds, then he untangled himself from her. The hint of a secretive smile tipped up his lips. "Let me move these boxes for you."

Gloria tilted her head to the side and wrinkled her nose. "I only need the top one for now."

He ignored her instructions and effortlessly transferred several boxes to the nearby trolly cart and pulled them out of the unit, revealing another set of boxes. A row of four boxes. Each labelled in black marker with one word.

Will

You

Marry

Me?

She swung back to Owen, who'd dropped down on one knee and now held out a modest diamond ring. "I know I let you down, and I know it'll happen again. I'm going to mess up, but I will never walk away from you. I will always fight for you. I will defend you."

Gloria moved her gaze over the face of the man she loved. The remnants of the last few difficult weeks carved crevices in the corners of his eyes and across his forehead. Her throat squeezed.

"Frank Brisbane once told me my wife only gets one husband and my kids only get one father, but the church can always hire a new pastor. I know that now in a way I didn't understand before."

Heat filled her chest, cheeks, and head. *His kids. Her kids. Their kids.*

"This is probably not the romantic proposal you've dreamt of your whole life—"

Wrong.

"—but I didn't want to share this moment with anyone else—"

She tried not to think about who might be in the car crawling down the nearby road at a snail's pace.

"—in a town like ours, this is pretty much the only place I could be sure we'd be alone, and privacy trumped romance."

Oh, this was romantic, all right.

He cleared his throat, but instead of reading the script he'd scrawled onto the boxes behind her, he launched into rhyme.

"When life pours me lemons, I'll think lemonade.
When the sun gets too hot, I'll be thankful for shade."

Her eyes tingled. She blinked fast. Her gaze zipped to the open box that held her preschool materials, and sure enough, her favorite book was missing.

A secretive grin snaked across Owen's face.

"No matter how awful or ugly it gets,
I can be thankful for something, I'd bet."

He'd memorized her poem. *He'd memorized her poem. HE'D MEMORIZED HER POEM.* Pressure grew behind her eyes.

Owen never broke eye contact.

"You are the you that you need to be.
No one else can be you, no one else, no siree.
If I didn't have you, I'd be missing a lot.

You matter. You're wanted. Your company's sought."

She blinked, and dampness spilled over her cheeks.

"Be true to what's you, be you all the way.
They can't take from you what you won't give away."

His voice cracked. The last few words tripped over one another, but he'd never sounded so eloquent. She couldn't breathe. She couldn't speak. But she could remember.

That first raspberry kiss in the clearing behind the church. Their first date. Owen taking her to prom and slipping that ridiculously huge corsage onto her wrist. Standing with her against the town, declaring her to be honest and upright when Tiff claimed the opposite. Not pushing when she pulled back. Giving her space when she retreated. Seeking her out when she tried to return to town in secret. Calling in Ben and Emma to carry on the task of exposing Emergence when she couldn't. Driving to the city to see her and take her on dates. Eating soup from a can so he could treat her to dinner. Standing up for her when her character was challenged. Loving her when she wasn't being loveable. Loving her like Christ loved His church. Owen would give his life for her. She had no doubt.

He had not failed her. Never.

"Gloria Sycamore, will you marry me?"

With a gulp and a short cry, she hurtled toward him.

"Yes!" She buried her face into the curve of his neck and inhaled his familiar scent. She held it deep in her lungs. "Yes," she repeated. "Yes, I'll marry you."

Owen pulled back just far enough to slip the diamond onto her finger, and they stared at the representation of his promise to her. "I love you."

All tension of the previous weeks drained away, and he pressed his lips against hers in the sweetest, most chaste, most wonderful kiss ever. They lingered like that, both anticipating all the Lord had for them in the future. Eventually, Owen pulled back. He rubbed his hands up and down her arms, creating delicious friction. "You're trembling. Are you okay?"

She nodded. After all that had happened, she knew, beyond a shadow of a doubt, she was not a worthy woman, but that was okay. God loved the unworthy. He sent His Son to redeem the unworthy, and He made them worthy through Christ. "I'm more than okay."

God had replaced her shame with honor.

The Sycamore Slopes

BOOK 3

Follow Ben and Emma's story in The Sycamore Slopes as they try to unite the split town before an avalanche of trouble buries them.

CHAPTER ONE - THE SYCAMORE SLOPES

A bloodcurdling shriek sliced through the air. Ben Swayer didn't flinch. He merely lifted his camera, peered through the lens, and rotated the focusing ring. He concentrated on Sycamore Hill's ice-covered pond, the origin of the happy squeals. Skaters glided into the frame, and he held down the shutter release to utilize the camera's continuous shooting mode—a trick a fellow reporter taught him. Small-town newspapers didn't have the budget for photographers. The reporters pulled double duty.

Local Kids Glide Toward Better Health. Not the best

headline, but it'd have to do. The assignment editor threw this at Ben last minute. He thought an article on the town's outdoor activities paired well with Ben's exposé on the rising statistics of childhood obesity. Ben captured another cluster of images. The story wasn't a lead. Not even a shocker. It might as well be printed in the classifieds.

A chilly breeze pushed the scent of hot chocolate and corn dogs from a cluster of nearby food trucks. The sweet aroma dominated over sweaty bodies stuffed into winter snow suits. *Pop Up Food Vendors. Who Moderates Them?* Still boring, but he committed the potential headline to memory anyway.

Ben adjusted the camera lens again. The nip in the air reddened noses and chapped cheeks, but it colored no one more adorably than little Oliver, Kim Jansen's son. Kim had only recently regained custody of Oliver after her ex had spirited him out of the country. Ben covered the mother/son reunion for the paper, which was spearheaded by Oliver's Uncle Jackson.

Kim and Jackson sandwiched Oliver, clutching his mittened hands and supporting him on his skates. The average person would never guess all they had endured to get to this happy spot. But that's the way it often was. People only saw the outside. Scars lived underneath.

The blades slipped and slid beneath the boy. Oliver's face scrunched as if he were trying to climb Mount Everest. "I do it! I do it!"

Ben snapped another picture. *Local Boy Learns to*

Skate. Cute kids dominated the front pages of Sycamore Hill's paper. This one was sure to score Ben a place above the fold, but it was hardly the exclusive that jump-started a career. He'd already written that exclusive, and it got him nowhere.

A rope of kids linked hands to play crack the whip on the far side of the pond. Janelle Holmes, his neighbor's kid, squealed. The momentum of the skaters pulled the unfortunate tail over the surface of the ice.

Ben pivoted again. He zoomed in on the adjacent slope. Slope was a bit of a stretch, but it was the closest thing to a sledding hill the town could offer. Children slogged up the gentle incline, dragging sleds and plastic carpets behind them. Their friends zipped down the steep side in a strange conveyer belt of activity. He captured another grouping of images. *Fun on the Sycamore Slopes.* That should be enough.

But not Pulitzer Prize enough.

He navigated through the pictures, zooming in on faces, deleting the ones with closed eyes or unflattering angles. People liked seeing their photos in the paper, but only if their likeness complimented them. And parents loved seeing their children in print. He had enough shots of delighted youngsters for his bland assignment. Done with a capital D.

He repacked his satchel and squinted against the early pangs of a headache. The boughs of a frost-dusted pine tree blurred as he rubbed the butt of his palm in circles on his forehead. Could a career reporting for

Sycamore News make him happy? Just the idea of covering common occurrences for the rest of his life made his limbs heavy. Everything required an astronomical effort. Even his lungs resisted inflating.

"Uncle Ben!" Nico waved as he raced toward the hill. A long, blue sled attached to a thin, yellow rope bounced behind him.

The iceberg in his chest liquified. This was why he stayed. He wanted to watch his nephew grow up. He wanted to help his sister, Claire. He wanted to be here for his parents. But mostly, he wanted to make things permanent with Emma. He had the ring hidden in his bedside table. All he needed now was a plan. Nobody just proposed anymore.

"Look out!"

The panicked cry lifted the head of every adult. Ben swung, fumbling for his camera. Never pack the camera! Rookie mistake.

Powerful momentum sent Janelle on a trajectory toward Oliver. The ten-year-old girl's impact forced Oliver from Jackson and Kim's grip in seemingly slow motion. The boy catapulted into the air like a bull's prey and came down even harder with a thwack.

Silence fell just as spectacularly. Too quiet. Oliver should be crying.

No, no, no. No. NO.

This kind of quiet screamed everything was not okay. It roared in Ben's ears. Everything was not fine. Everything might never be fine again. He called Emma.

Ben pushed through the cluster of people. Jackson's hands roamed each little limb, and Kim cradled Oliver's head, not moving his neck.

Janelle had crumpled onto the ice off to the side. Her elbows pressed into her body. "I'm sorry! I'm sorry!"

"I called Emma." Ben dropped to a knee beside Jackson. "She'll be here any second."

The tendons in Jackson's neck popped out as he nodded. "Keep his head stabilized, Kim."

As the only police presence in town, Jackson was the next best thing to Emma. And as the only nurse practitioner in a town with no doctors, Emma was the next best thing to a paramedic or hospital. Ben's fisted hand bounced against his thigh. She should be here by now.

Oliver roused. He tried to move.

Ben craned his neck to scour the line of parked cars on the side road looking for Emma's familiar hatchback. *Come on, Emma.*

Kim leaned over Oliver so he could see her face. "Stay still, baby. You'll be okay." Oliver's knitted red hat absorbed Kim's tears.

Ben smeared the sweat beading on his lips across his cheeks. Traumas that involved children— They changed you. He sucked in and held his breath.

He was not thinking about that.

Kim pressed her lips to Oliver's forehead, still stabilizing him and murmuring soft words.

She sounded just like his mother had.

Emma medical's bag thudded onto the ice beside Ben,

jolting him from the past. He didn't even remember kneeling beside the boy, but his pant legs were soaked through. Emma checked Oliver's vitals. Her slender fingers moved his body. A long, auburn braid fell over one shoulder, and her knitted toque had been knocked askew. The bright striped pattern of blue and red contrasted with her creamy skin. Her clear eyes fixed on Oliver. "How long was he out?"

Kim pinched her lips. "Just a few minutes."

Seemingly satisfied that nothing was broken, Emma flicked a tiny penlight across Oliver's eyes. What she saw must have pleased her. As the stiffness in her posture loosened, Ben's relief shot out like a bullet.

Emma held Kim's gaze. "I think he'll be fine, but I'd like to take him to the clinic for a more thorough check up."

Kim wiped her eyes and reached for Jackson with a shaky hand. "Thank you."

"Can I carry him?" Jackson hovered, ready to scoop the boy up but unwilling to move him until Emma gave the okay.

She nodded.

Jackson tenderly carried the child to Kim's van. Jackson was one of the good guys. The kind of police officer children could trust. Like the one that returned Ben to his parents when he was lost as a child.

Not like the other officer. Not like the one that took him away. Ben stretched his cramped his fingers, flexing them at his sides.

Ben caught words and phrases like *champ, be brave, you'll be okay,* and *I've got you.* Jackson's optimistic tone and word choices contrasted with his sickly white complexion. The man loved that kid like a father.

"What took so long?" Ben shuffled closer to Emma as her attention shifted to Janelle.

Janelle's hands jammed into her armpits, and she rocked back and forth. Shallow breath sounds. Catatonic gaze.

Emma flicked her gaze to Ben, but instead of bouncing back to Janelle, she lingered. "I couldn't find a place to park." Her chin lifted to the right, and her head tilted. "Are you okay? You look pale."

Ben flattened his lips. The parking situation had become ridiculous. The pond and the slope jetted off a dead-end street. Vehicles filled the nearby side roads, many of them blocking the resident's driveways. "I'll be fine. But Janelle's not looking so good."

Emma knelt in front of Janelle. She patiently waited for Janelle to lift her head. The circumference of the dark circle growing over Emma's denim-clad knees increased. She kept her hands still.

Finally, Janelle made eye contact.

"Are you hurt?"

Janelle shook her head. "Is Oliver gonna be okay?"

"I think so. How are you?"

Janelle blinked. At some point, her hat had fallen off, and static electricity lifted strands of dark hair.

"I'm fine." Janelle cut her eyes to Ben. "Is this going to be in the paper?"

He started to say no but stopped. He'd been sent to report on the activities. The editor might divert to winter safety once he heard of the accident. "I don't know. But I won't take your picture unless you want me to." That, he could promise.

"I don't."

Ben patted his satchel. "Then my camera stays put."

"Can I check you over?" Emma placed a gentle hand on Janelle's shoulder.

Emma's soft mannerisms had a calming effect. Ben's erratic pulse normalized. Emma was not the doctor that made a terrible mistake. Jackson was not the police officer that took Ben away from his parents. Everything was going to be fine.

Janelle tugged her jacket sleeves down over her gloved hands. "I'm okay."

"I expect you are, but I'd like to be sure. Sometimes shock stops us from feeling everything."

Janelle nodded a curt consent.

Emma completed a basic examination and then sat back on her heels. "You're right. You seem fine. But I'll call your parents so they can keep an eye on you."

Janelle diverted her gaze.

Interesting. Was she afraid they'd be angry at her? Ben had never seen or heard anything concerning from his neighbor's house.

Emma repacked her emergency medical kit and hoisted herself to her feet. Her damp knees didn't seem to bother her. "I better get to the clinic. Oliver will be waiting."

Ben clutched the top of his satchel to camouflage the shakiness in his hands. "You have to fill out an incident report, right?"

She nodded.

"I saw the accident. It wasn't Kim or Jackson's fault. I want to add my testimony to the paperwork."

A tiny laugh bubbled from Emma. Not a laugh of mockery. She wasn't the type to poke fun. It was more like a chuckle of relief. She started to walk toward the side road where she must have parked, although he still couldn't see her vehicle. "That's not necessary. I'll make a note it was an ice-skating accident. It's no big deal."

Ben didn't remember the doctor's exact words to his mother, but they were probably similar and spoken in the same casual tone. The doctor had no idea that his belief in the system would rip Ben's family apart. Emma stood at the edge of the same cliff, and another family teetered on the precipice. "It's a big deal for me. I want to be sure everything is noted. You know, for later, if necessary."

Emma stopped and faced Ben, fisting her hands on her hips. Her eyebrows pulled together, and her nose wrinkled adorably. "Did something happen that you're not telling me?"

He avoided her eyes. He wasn't ready. He might

never be ready. "If you have legal responsibilities to report certain types of injuries, I just want to be there."

She studied him for a second longer before conceding. "You're a sweet man for caring so much." She lifted onto her tiptoes and pressed a chaste kiss to his lips.

An unexpected release of tension loosened the knots in Ben's neck. He wasn't sure whether it was relief over not needing to explain why this mattered so much or her yielding to his request. But either way, justice would prevail.

"Thank you. I'll be there as soon as I can." He lightly squeezed her hands as she pulled away.

She gave him a playful wink. "Don't be long."

Now the excitement was over, skaters had returned to the ice. They twirled and held hands. Blades scraped the frozen surface, mixing with laughter and innocent squealing. Life went on.

Someone pressed play on their winter playlist, but it couldn't quite smother the songs of childhood. Ben wanted this for his kids. A community. A place to belong. A place that stood together.

His imaginary kids.

An increasing warmth in his chest warred with his cold toes. Emma had reached her car, tucked between two vans. She turned for a final wave, disappeared inside, and drove off. He and Emma hadn't discussed children yet. They hadn't even discussed marriage, although that was where their track headed. At least it was where he hoped it was headed. They'd reached what his mom called "the ripe age of early thirties," and according to her, their train raced to the tick of a biological clock.

His career ran alongside that train on a parallel track. At least, it was parallel until Grander City Daily News offered him a job. It wasn't the hard-hitting journalism he once dreamed of, but it was a step up from Sycamore Hill. The only catch was they required him to move to the city. Emma had worked too hard to become a nurse practitioner and open her medical clinic to follow him to the city. He'd have to choose.

He'd worked his whole life for an opportunity to report at a big city paper and stir the poisonous pots the government had its hands in. But now that a paper had reached out, his feet got cold. Ben stomped his size twelve boots, and they sunk into the snow. A frosty tingle crept toward his ankles.

He couldn't think about that right now. Protecting Oliver was all that mattered. The poor kid had already suffered enough in his young life. Ben would write an article that mentioned the accident. It ensured the truth was officially recorded somewhere. It was an accident. And someone other than the doctor and police needed to know.

Accidents happened. This wasn't anybody's fault.

The winter activities of sledding, pond skating, and skiing keep nurse practitioner Emma Powles busy in her newly-established medical clinic. They also divide the town when a local boy is injured. All Nico wants is to conquer the Sycamore Slope, something Emma encourages him to attempt. But instead of battling against the grumpy old Grinch trying to ban the activities, her strongest opponent is the one person she believed would always side with her.

Ben Sawyer, a local reporter, has vowed to protect the vulnerable from corrupt authorities. His nephew's injury inflames traumatic memories and a personal bias that can't stop the descending danger as the fight to control Sycamore Hill heats up. Battle lines are drawn, and a big city newspaper follows Ben's coverage. However, the cost of professional success might be more than he is willing to pay.

Will Emma and Ben unite the split town before an avalanche of trouble buries them?

Order now!

One Sycamore Sunday

BOOK 4

What began as a normal Sunday changed Kim and
Jackson's lives forever.

A Sycamore Secret

BOOK 5

Mixing a tenacious morning show host with a decades-old secret is a recipe for disaster.

To Sweet Beginnings in Sycamore Hill

SERIES INTRODUCTION

SEE HOW IT ALL BEGAN FOR THE COUPLES YOU LOVE FROM SYCAMORE HILL.

When a whistleblower speaks up, she tips the first domino of a twenty-four-hour chain reaction on the eve of Sycamore Hill's most important holiday event. A baker gets a career-making opportunity, a reporter chases the truth, a woman faces her greatest fear, and a lost child returns as the dominos continue to fall. The residents of Sycamore Hill approach a new year, and five couples celebrate sweet beginnings filled with endless possibilities in this short story sequence.

Order now!

OWEN AND GLORIA: THURSDAY 2:00 P.M.

Sycamore Hill's prodigal daughter returns, shaking up the small town, righting a wrong, and finding the faith and family she'd lost along the way.

Gloria hasn't returned to Sycamore Hill since her university declared her guilty of cheating. She'd lost more than her home that day; she'd lost her faith in humanity. But when a questionable drug study with ties to the university endangers the residents of a Sycamore Hill ministry, Gloria can no longer remain quiet. She returns to town, and Owen—the town's unmarried pastor and the only person who believed in her innocence—helps her to finally and truly come home.

ETHAN AND KATHRYN: THURSDAY 11:59 P.M.

When you mix two former sweethearts, one missing recipe, and a dash of secrecy, what do you get? A recipe for romance!

Kathryn took something that belongs to Ethan. Correction. It belongs to his family. Taking it back isn't stealing, and letting himself into Kathryn's house to get it is not breaking and entering if he has a key. However, Kathryn's not a thief. She'd found Ethan's recipe. But when her actions threaten to spoil Ethan's bakery, they whip up a solution on Kathryn's internet morning show, Sycamore Hill at Sunrise.

BEN AND EMMA: FRIDAY 3:00 A.M.

God closes a door, but He opens a skylight, entwining Ben and Emma's future in the twilight hours of a winter's eve.

Nursing school made dating impossible for Emma, and now that she finally has time to think about a relationship, the pickings are slim, especially in a small town like Sycamore Hill. She's begun petitioning the Lord to drop Mr. Right into her life, ideally before a black-tie gala fundraiser. She can't bear the idea of attending alone —again.

When Ben—a local reporter—chases the scoop of a lifetime, he falls painfully into Emma's kitchen. With a whistleblower about to rip the lid off a scandal that'll put the small town on the map, Ben needs Emma's help to follow the career-making lead and protect the residents of Sycamore Hill.

ELI AND MEG: FRIDAY 7:35 A.M.

At some point, a girl has to stop running and fight. Eli is willing to help Meg, but how can he fight an unknown enemy?

Eli and Meg trained together every morning to prepare for an annual road race. When Meg is uncharacteristically late on race day, Eli knows in his gut that something is wrong. He finds Meg facing her greatest fear, and Eli thrusts himself between her and an aggressive animal. However, when Meg passes up an opportunity to escape to safety, he realizes no one in Sycamore Hill really knows Meg at all.

JACKSON AND KIM: FRIDAY, 6:00 P.M. AND SATURDAY MORNING

Kim didn't want to like her ex's twin brother, but how could she not like the man returning her abducted son?

Kim doesn't have the mental headspace to host the black-tie gala on the eve of her abducted son's homecoming, but she must. As she grapples with conflicting emotions about the morning reunion, she clings to the message of Christmas: God with us.

Returning his nephew to Canada destroyed Jackson's relationship with his twin brother. And after all his brother had put Kim through, she might not welcome the continued presence of Jackson or his parents in

Sycamore Hill. Sorting out the legalities won't be easy, but the right thing rarely is. Jackson will do what is right, whatever the personal cost, trusting the message of the season.

Order now!

The Sycamore Standoff

BOOK 1

Eli and Meg's story continues in The Sycamore Standoff, where Meg wants independence and Eli wants her affections. They'll have to face her past for any chance of a future.

She wants independence. He wants her affections.
They'll have to face her past for any chance of a future.

———

Meg Gilmore escapes an abusive relationship and rebuilds her life, but her victory is short-lived. Change threatens her new refuge, and she underestimates her adversary. But Meg is a fighter. She will do whatever it takes to protect what she loves. Her past catches up with her present and uproots everything she has built, including a fragile and growing friendship with a kind and generous man. The freedom and love Meg has always wanted is hers for the taking, but she'll have to confront what truly terrifies her to claim it.

Order your copy!

Glorious Surrender

NON-FICTION

Finding the treasure hidden in trials.

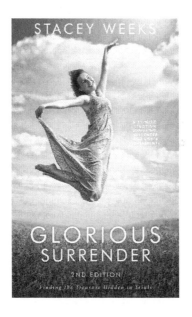

Do you long for the joy of complete dependence on God yet fear the cost of full surrender? Do you long for unconditional acceptance and love but fear exposing your heart? Do you long for solid peace, absolute trust, and contentment amidst alarming circumstances but fear that those circumstances might shatter your soul?

We fight God for control of our lives because we worry that suffering will overwhelm us. We want a future free of risk, hurt, and heartbreak. But God isn't calling us to risk-free lives

—He is calling us to surrender. Some of God's greatest blessings are hiding behind those parts of our lives that are most difficult to surrender.

The first edition won the Women's Journey of Faith award. The second edition of Glorious Surrender includes five personal, in-depth study times in the Word to aid in the application and understanding of Scripture.

PRAISE FOR GLORIOUS SURRENDER

In Glorious Surrender, Stacey Weeks writes with transparency about the tension and the transformation that her role as a pastor's wife played in bringing her to the place of ultimate freedom—one who seeks God's glory above all else. She communicates with honesty about the messiness of real life in public ministry and takes readers on a journey through raw life topics including pride, living authentically, finding true rest in the chaos, and spiritual warfare. Her passion for God's glory to preoccupy and transform everyday living accompanies every thought on every page. This book is not just for pastors' wives, it is for women wanting to take a vulnerable look at the sins and deceptions that lurk within their minds and hearts that can stall their progress toward finding true purpose. A must-read!

— ANDREA THOM, AUTHOR OF

RUTH: REDEEMING THE DARKNESS
AND AMOS: COME AWAKE!

Often we sit in our seats and wonder what the life of our pastor is like but forget that there is another person in that relationship that must honour the God-given calling of that man. Glorious Surrender is more than Stacey's story; it is about God's ability to shape any ordinary person into the image of Him.

— KEVIN MILLER, CHURCH ELDER

If you want to glorify God in everything you think, say, and do, I recommend reading Glorious Surrender.

— TAMI SWARTZ, BIBLICAL COUNSELLOR

Chasing Holiness

NON-FICTION

Spend seven weeks learning how to live by the power of God and cultivate a lifestyle in keeping with who you really are in Christ.

We all chase something. It might be a degree or career, a husband and family, the approval of man, or a perception of social success. We long to pursue the things that matter, we long to chase the Lord, but we are weary. What would happen if we redirected our energy toward developing the character traits and disciplines that Christ calls us to pursue? What if we sought ways to increase our endurance and strengthen our faith? What if we stopped aimlessly running and instead chased the disciplines that would earn the prize that mattered?

Chasing Holiness challenges the status quo level of Christian living accepted for far too long by many women today. It's about teaching stubborn hearts through the discipline of seeking God to remain focused on Him. It examines what it means to live by the power of God and believe Him when He calls us a daughter, chosen, holy, and redeemed. It encourages women to cultivate a lifestyle in keeping with who we really are in Christ. It's an acknowledgment that many of us long to fix our eyes on Jesus and push toward the finish line, but we don't know where to start. Chasing Holiness is about finding out together.

PRAISE FOR CHASING HOLINESS

"Stacey's style of writing guides the not-yet believer gently, informs the recent believer, and challenges the mature believer toward the desire for all Christians — holiness. Themes of doctrine, Scripture, and day-to-day life with its struggles are presented as understandable and relatable to the reader. One isn't left feeling inadequate but rather inspired to chase after holiness as a result of reading this work."

— LAURA COLWELL - DIRECTOR OF WOMEN'S MINISTRY, HOPE BIBLE CHURCH, OAKVILLE ONTARIO

"I want every woman in our church to read and study *Chasing Holiness*. There is nothing easy about

Stacey's words. This is a clear and necessary call to holy living. A call that is sadly absent from many pulpits and "Christian" books today. With honesty and transparency, Stacey shares from her own life but not in that I've-got-it-all-figured-out kind of way. The reader will feel the connection and be moved into the chase with her. The book is saturated with Scripture, moving from powerful explanations of the biblical texts to application that is simple and accessible. The study questions at the end of each chapter, Bible study group plan, and list of additional resources make this a must-have book for women who are serious about their walk with Christ."

— TODD DUGARD, LEAD PASTOR - HARVEST BIBLE CHAPEL, BARRIE ONTARIO

"Foundational to Christian living is a proper knowledge of God and responding submissively and completely. This study blends biblical insight with practical reflection to help move us forward in our intimacy with Jesus."

— ANDREA THOM - BIBLE TEACHER, AUTHOR OF RUTH: REDEEMING THE DARKNESS AND AMOS: COME AWAKE

"Stacey Weeks accurately identifies a massively concerning issue in today's church culture. We long for Jesus but we risk missing Him all together. This is why this timely book is a must-read for Christian women who are hungry to grow and faithfully follow Christ. Far too many are missing not just the truth, but literally missing Him! Take Stacey's charge to heart; read, study, pray about, and share this book for "He is worthy of pursuing, so Chase Holiness!"

— NORM MILLAR -SENIOR PASTOR - REDEMPTION BIBLE CHAPEL, LONDON ONTARIO

"Paul talks about running the race with endurance, but that can often feel quite ambiguous. Stacey takes you on a journey through the Word of God, helping you ask the right questions; that you might not just "know" the importance of holiness, but understand how to practice, pursue, and even chase holiness intentionally. I can't wait to go through the study with some of the women in my life as we walk this path in His Spirit and to His glory together!"

— LAURA ZIMMERMAN - DIRECTOR OF PROJECTS AND EVENTS, GREAT COMMISSION COLLECTIVE

"I love this book! I value its conviction. I agree with its goal, and I wholeheartedly support its theology. In a day of *hamster wheel* chaotic lives in pursuit of the temporal, the call to chase after holiness is joyfully welcomed. Actually, desperately needed. Weeks writes with clarity, sincerity, and honesty that is easy to digest and then powerfully apply. Read this book, but don't rush through this book. When you truly comprehend its message, your life will see God's path, know His power, and experience His purity. It's that important."

— ROBBIE SYMONS, AUTHOR OF PASSION CRY, PASTOR OF HOPE BIBLE CHURCH, OAKVILLE ONTARIO

Acknowledgments

Writing is never a one-person adventure. Despite the hours I live inside my head working on a story or book, countless others invest in the project. I would have never created Sycamore Hill without the encouragement of my writing friends in the Brantford Writers Group. Thank you, Karen, Sandy, Heather, Tara, and Deirdre for your enthusiasm and belief in me. You believed these characters had more to their stories.

Thank you to an extraordinary editor, Olivia, from LivEdits. You helped tie the threads of this story together. I look forward to our next project together.

About the Author

———

Stacey is a ministry wife, mother of three teenagers, and a sipper of hot tea with honey. She loves to open the Word of God and share the hope of Christ with women. She is a multi-award-winning author, the primary home-educator of her children, and a frequent conference speaker. Her messages have been described as rich in the truths of Scripture, gospel-infused, and life-changing. Stacey has a Graduate Certificate in Women's Ministry from Heritage College and Seminary and is working toward a Graduate Certificate in Biblical Counselling.

facebook.com/writerSWeeks

twitter.com/writerSWeeks

instagram.com/writerSWeeks

You Can Make a Difference

REVIEW HIS SYCAMORE SWEETHEART

Did you enjoy this book? You can make a difference. Honest reviews of books bring them to the attention of other readers. If you enjoyed this book, I would be grateful if you could take a few minutes to leave an online review or star rating where you purchased the book. You can also post reviews and star ratings on Goodreads and Bookbub.

Manufactured by Amazon.ca
Bolton, ON

27952626R00114